Who *WAS* the second wife of Dr. John H. Watson, trusted friend and associate of the legendary Sherlock Holmes? Sir Arthur Conan Doyle only hinted at her existence, launching a literary mystery that is still debated to this day.

The secret is now revealed in "The Adventures of the Second Mrs. Watson," a collection of twelve stories featuring Amelia Watson, the devoted, intrepid, and highly opinionated spouse of the good Dr. Watson. These lighthearted and evocative tales follow Amelia over two continents as she is thrust into baffling mystery after mystery, in which she often finds herself at odds with the great Mr. Holmes himself.

Think you know everything about Sherlock Holmes? Think again, because now Amelia Watson is on the case, and the "game" will never be quite the same again!

THE ADVENTURES OF THE SECOND MRS. WATSON

by Michael Mallory

For Era

Enjoy!

Best,

Michael Mallory

DEADLY ALIBI PRESS LTD.

Deadly Alibi Press Ltd.
PO Box 5947
Vancouver, WA 98668-5947

Library of Congress Catalog Card Number: 9966064

ISBN: 1-886199-06-X (Acid free paper)

TABLE OF CONTENTS

For Margo, without whom these stories
would not have been;

And for Helen, without whom I would
not be.

I find from my notebook that it was January, 1903, just after the conclusion of the Boer War...The good Watson had at that time deserted me for a wife, the only selfish action which I can recall in our association.

Mr. Sherlock Holmes, from:
"The Adventure of the Blanched Soldier" by A. Conan Doyle

THE ADVENTURE OF
THE LEFT-BEHIND WIFE

Letter to Mrs. Elizabeth Newington from
Mrs. Amelia Watson   July 19, 1903

My dearest Beth —

Forgive me for not having returned your correspondence until now, but John was ill recently. Nothing serious, but for a medical man he takes notoriously little care of himself, and he should really know better than to stay up the entire evening hidden in a hedge, playing out some *Boys Own Detective* adventure yet again. Yes, Beth, I am afraid that I must report that the 'boys' are at it again — John and that demented friend of his. I tell John that he is entirely too old for this sort of nonsense — 51 on his next birthday — but he does not listen. Why should he, after all, I am only his wife; and, as he so frequently points out to me, merely a *woman*. I begin to fear, Beth, that he has clung to that prig Holmes for so long, and has had his ego punctured so often by this same companion of choice, that he can only justify his manhood by putting me in my place as "merely a woman."

Yet I hope I do not sound unduly harsh towards John. He really can be a dear; kind and warmhearted, as you well know, and all too willing to do a worthy deed for any needy person who cannot pay (if it were not for his military pension, Beth, I should probably have to scrub floors to support us). And I have great reason to feel soft towards him at present — but more of that later.

What I really want to tell you is that I have finally met the 'great man' himself. Prior to this I have known him only through John's magazine stories, which tend to colour reality in hues that would have embarrassed Oscar Wilde's tailor, and through his incessant speaking of him. It is "Holmes, Holmes, Holmes," all day long and into the evening, as if no one else exists. But I begin to digress. Let me tell you of the singular (to use John's favourite word) events that lead up to my meeting the world's foremost consulting detective Mr. Sherlock Holmes.

(And Beth, be honest — have you ever known anyone else on earth named *Sherlock*?)

How would John put it, let's see...It was on a bleak grey morning in the spring of the year when London was in the grip of a persistent, many-tentacled fog (how am I doing so far, dear?) that I first saw the old match-selling woman.

That morning my husband, Dr. John H. Watson, had no sooner sat down to breakfast in our small but comfortable flat when a rather grimy youth appeared at the door, message-in-hand. A message for John delivered in such fashion means one of two things: He is required immediately for a medical emergency or the game is once more afoot. Alas, it was the latter.

The change that comes over him whenever he reads a summons from his friend, Mr. Sherlock Holmes, is quite remarkable. He loses all appetite immediately, leaps up from the table and begins prancing around with great agitation. His eyes take on new light, and while some may think me mad for saying so, I swear that the grey in his hair actually streaks back to its natural brown and he becomes once again a callow youth wild for adventure.

"Holmes needs me, my dear," he said excitedly, racing to his desk and burrowing through the files heaped upon it until he had found his Bradshaw's. Please believe me, Beth, that my heart sinks at the very sight of that railway schedule.

"You are not leaving town, again?" I asked plaintively, to which he replied, "I am very sorry, my dear, but this is something urgent. That was Holmes' very word, *urgent*." Opening a desk drawer, John withdrew his old service revolver.

"John!"

"Hmm? Oh, don't worry, Amelia, I do not expect to have to use this. I carry it because...well, I carry it because I feel almost like I am missing a limb without it. I suppose you could call it a habit."

Two grown men, two habits: One injects himself with cocaine while the other plays with guns. I tell you, Beth, it is a wonder they are both still alive.

The most distressing act was when he pulled down his battered suitcase and began throwing clean shirts into it, a week's worth at least, ruining whatever press they might once have possessed.

"Oh, John, how long will you be gone this time?"

"I cannot say, my dear, but I shall write to you. Do not worry, my love. I shall be fine." Yes, *he* would be fine.

Throwing his hat on...backwards...he raced for the stairs and I followed. "What if a patient comes?"

"Refer them to Dr. Fennyman, as usual. Good bye, my dear." And out he went.

Do you know, Beth, that last month we actually received a thank you note from Dr. Fennyman, so improved has his practice become because of John's running off with Holmes?

Once again left to finish breakfast alone, I tried to read the Times but it meant nothing. Words are only words if you cannot concentrate on the idea behind them, and at that moment the only thing I could concentrate on was the loss of my husband to a misanthropic mistress named Sherlock Holmes.

But I had not long to wait before the adventure began.

Deciding to take a stroll along the street (however gloomy it was outside, it was gloomier still in the quiet flat) and perhaps get in a bit of shopping, I bundled up against the misty chill and went out. I had not even set foot on the sidewalk when I saw her.

Do you remember, Beth, back in the theatre there was a fellow who played nothing but walk-ons, spear carriers or towns-people, rarely ever getting the chance to read a line? I can't recall his name, but I'm sure you will remember him because we used to make such fun of his ability to be seen. No matter how insignificant his role, and no matter how vital it was that he blend into a crowd, this fellow would stand out by his too-careful attempt to appear inconsequential; rather than being a part of a crowd, he acted the role of a man who was a part of a crowd, and stood out like a black eye. Thus it was with this woman.

She was old and bent, and appeared to be the proprietress of a match booth, but there was something about her which was not right. In trying to become a part of the street she fussed and fidgeted and did any number of old womanly things, all of which appeared to my eyes to be a little too carefully rehearsed. However, figuring that this was her selling technique, making herself just a bit older and more feeble than she actually was to gain additional buyer sympathy, I gave the crone no more thought and went about my business.

I shall not bore you with the details of my expedition, except to say that nothing in the stores suited me that day. I was just starting the journey home when I saw her again, standing at the corner near the shop, advertising her wares in a flat, shrill sing-song voice and blessing the few who actually passed a half-penny her way. My immediate reaction was that this strange woman had followed me, yet why on earth would she do so? Could I simply be imagining things? Or had I let the perpetual talk of mystery and mayhem that flurries around our home like winter's snow melt into my head?

Paying no attention to the woman — who indeed, seemed to pay no attention to me — I made my way back and did not encounter her again.

The evening was long and sleepless, as it usually is when John is off playing, and I awoke the next morning is a poor mood; uncomfortable and not a little bit angry. How dare he keep running off at a moment's notice with no consideration towards me, and little towards the patients who have come to depend upon him!

The morning's post brought his promised letter, but I waited before opening it, letting myself cool down somewhat. As usually happens, the anger subsided and gave way to the dull ache of loneliness. I married John because I wanted to be with him, and I presumed that he wanted to be with me as well.

His note placed him at Henley-on-Thames, of all places, and said very little else except that his new 'mission' was a vital one and that he missed my presence. Oh, John...dear, sweet, guileless John...

I had already decided to venture forth that day, having found nothing within the flat to keep me occupied for another solitary afternoon, and glanced out of the window to check the weather. Immediately I saw that she was back, the old match-seller. Only this time, I caught her looking directly at our window, just for the tiniest fleeting moment. Whoever this woman was, and whatever her purpose, I was now convinced that she was watching me.

As you well know, Beth, I am not a person who is easily rattled or whose nerves are close to the surface, but this strange haggard woman, dressed in black rags, innocuously peddling her matches while keeping a close watch of my movements, unnerved me greatly. I cancelled all plans to leave the premises and instead attempted to teach the game of chess to Missy, our new young maid, who looked upon the prospect of ceasing her duties for an afternoon of amusement as the greatest thing that had ever happened to her.

I remained inside the next day as well, having received my daily dispatch from John, vague as usual, but a touch more affectionate, and I was quite relieved to notice that the old match-seller was nowhere to be seen from our window. My relief was short-lived, however, with the appearance of Missy in our chambers, an odd expression on her face. "Ma'am, there is a woman here to see the doctor."

"The doctor is away, please give her the address of Dr. Fennyman."

"Yes'm, I tried to do that, but she wouldn't listen. She says it's to be Dr. Watson or no one."

Before I could speak to reply, "It must be no one then," another voice was heard outside the door — a shrill, high, wheezy voice.

"Doctor Watson did me a good turn onest, he did, soes its Dr. Watson I wants ter see."

The woman bustled her way in past Missy before either of us could object. Her tray of matches was gone, but she wore the same black ragged dress and shawl in which I has seen her the past two days. The woman coughed violently then sank — nearly fell — into a chair.

"Get some water, Missy," I called, and when she had left to fetch it I approached the woman and asked: "What do you want with me?"

Blinking her bleary eyes as though trying to focus them, she wheezed: "Wit you, dearie? Oh, I don't want nottin' wit you. It's Doctor Watson I want."

As I came closer to her the entire plot suddenly became clear to me, as if a cloud had suddenly lifted and shown me the light. I say *plot*, because that is exactly what it was, Beth, a plot of the most devious sort. This woman, I now understood, had indeed been watching me, spying on me while John was away, and I was sure I knew why. When Missy returned with the water, I told her that the situation was well under control and sent her out.

"So, madam, it is Dr. Watson you want?" I said, and the old woman replied, "Yes, dearie, it's him what I wants."

"Well, I want him, too, Mr. Holmes!"

For the tiniest instant a look of total shock crossed the "old woman's" face, then it was gone again. Coughing loudly she said, "I don't knows whatcher mean?"

"Please, Mr. Holmes, do not insult my intelligence with this charade any longer. Tell me why you have sent my husband out of the city on some trumped-up cause so you can spy on me."

Suddenly the figure's demeanor changed completely. Rather than slumping in the chair, the 'old woman' sat up stiffly, 'her' cold grey eyes boring into mine. But believe me, Beth, I stared back with every ounce of my being, refusing to be intimidated. Finally 'she' said, "very well, madam," in a much deeper, more resonant voice, and began to peel away the layers of the match-seller; first the shawl and long grey hair, then the sharp beakish nose complete with a wart, then the dress itself. Underneath was a man I knew to be roughly fifty, but looking older, gaunt with thinning dark hair, wearing a plain shirt and thin trousers, the bottoms of which were rolled up so as not to show underneath the dress. He kept the old woman's square shoes on his feet. "May I smoke?" he asked curtly.

"Of course. Now please tell me what this is about, Mr. Holmes?"

"I will, but you must tell me something first," he said, nervously lighting up a cigarette. "How did you see through my disguise? Or was it just a lucky guess?"

I had such an urge at that moment to reply: *It was elementary*, but I managed to fight it down. "It was no guess, Mr. Holmes," I answered, "but in truth I did not see through it at all; I smelled through it?"

"I beg your pardon?"

"Your skill at makeup is quite remarkable, it lives up to every report John has written about it." Here he bowed his head slightly, acknowledging the compliment, and a small tight smile played on his lips. I went on: "But it was still obviously makeup. Anyone who has ever encountered greasepaint, nose wax and spirit gum knows that nothing on earth smells like it. When I got close enough to you to detect the scent of the makeup, I wondered why an old woman would wear theatrical cosmetics in public. Why would anyone, for that matter? Then I realized that there was only one person in London who would do so."

With a sudden movement Holmes banged himself on the forehead with the palm of his hand, spilling a good bit of ash on the furniture in the process. "Ah! What a fool I was! Of course! Watson told me you had been in amateur theatrics." (So John had actually mentioned me to the great Sherlock Holmes!)

"My congratulations on your successful deduction," he mumbled.

"Now it is your turn, Mr. Holmes. Why have you gone through all this? Why have you taken my husband away from me?"

"Because I wanted to meet the woman who had taken him away from *me*," he answered fiercely. "My rival for his affections, as it were."

At that moment, Beth, I did not know what to say. Of his complete sincerity there was no doubt, likewise his innocence; in his own way he loved my husband, though I doubt that word would have sprung to his mind. Immediately I saw the real Sherlock Holmes: an isolated and highly vulnerable man who had denied himself a good deal of what life had to offer in the pursuit of his profession, his "duty," as it were, and a man who had but one friend in the world — only one. And here I stood as the force that threatened to remove that friend.

"Madam, I am lost without my Boswell, can you understand that?" Holmes cried.

"I can try to, Mr. Holmes. Does John know that our meeting is taking place?"

"No, of course not. He is quite comfortable at a country inn in Henley, watching the other roomers like a hawk and reporting their every move to me. I have told him that a notorious international jewel thief is expected to pass through the area and have asked that he watch for any unusual comings and goings. He, in turn, thinks I am at Bray, doing likewise. When the affair is over, I shall have recovered the jewels — here they are, as a matter of fact —" He reached into a pocket and brought out a dozen large and breathtaking gemstones. " — Yes, they are real; I captured the actual criminal last week. But at the end of this latest adventure, your good husband will have yet another exploit to write for the popular press, and will be the happier for it. So you see, madam, there is no harm done."

The way this man played with John's illusions — I was absolutely livid! "You see no harm in setting a man up to be a fool? What if he were to find out that you had sent him on this snipe hunt simply as a bizarre prank? What if he were to learn that you play him like a musical instrument, preying on his affections until you get just the right tune to suit you?"

"Madam, I give you my word that I have never done and never will do anything that will hurt him. I shall not tell him of this escapade, so if the good doctor does learn of it, it will be from other lips than mine."

"I shall not tell him either," I finally said quietly.

"Excellent!" He leapt out of the chair and snuffed out the butt of his cigarette in one of John's trays. "I came here to see what sort of woman would pull him away from me, and I have. A most remarkable sort, if I may be so blunt as to say so." One of those peculiar almost-smiles danced again on his lips.

"You could not have simply come to the door and announced yourself, I suppose?" I said.

"Ha! Madam, that would not have been part of the game, now, would it?"

Taking up the pieces of his disguise, Mr. Sherlock Holmes headed for the door.

"Don't keep him out too long," I said, and with a subtle laugh by way of reply, the man was gone.

John came home a day later, exhilarated of course, and itching to sit down at his writing desk to compose the new tale. Once again, it was "Holmes, Holmes, Holmes, Holmes, Holmes." But at least I had the satisfaction this time of knowing, or at least sensing, that when the two are out on one of their 'games,' Mr. Holmes is likewise treated to "Amelia, Amelia, Amelia, Amelia..." As I am sure my name will never appear in one of his fictions, I must content myself with that.

That would have been the end of the story, dear Beth, except for one last thing. Not a week later John was once again summoned by his friend, this time for lunch. I was not invited, of course. When John returned his expression was indescribable. I positively thought he was going to burst! He asked me to close my eyes and hold out my hand, and into it he placed a stunning, blue-white diamond, roughly the size of a sixpence! "Where on earth did you get this?" I asked, and breathlessly, he explained that it was reward for his and Holmes' capture of the jewel thief. Holmes had given it to him, he said, claiming that he had no use for it. "Perhaps you should pass it on to your new wife, Watson," he quoted Holmes as saying, "consider it a belated wedding present from yours truly."

It is amazing what a stone of that size and beauty does towards establishing a forgiving mood. I am wearing it in a ring as I write this, and thinking of dear John out gallivanting around the countryside with his peculiar friend, keeping the world safe from crime and villainy, real or imagined, and awaiting his return.

I am afraid I must leave you now, Beth, as Missy has come in for our nightly chess game. And do you know — that the little snip actually *won* yesterday? Really!

My best to Robert.
Yours ever,
Amelia.

THE ADVENTURE OF
THE OTHER WOMAN

"Great Scott, did you read this?" cried my husband, who was pouring over the London *Times* during his morning meal of kippered herring, a dish I positively loathe.

"What, John?" I replied, trying to remain out of the vacant dead gaze of that fish.

"It says here that the head of the figure of Mr. Sherlock Holmes has been stolen from Madam Tussaud's wax museum. What a singular occurrence; I wonder what it could mean?"

I used the occasion to have our maid, Missy, remove the offending ichthyolite from the table, since this newspaper account had obviously signalled the end of John's breakfast. I, however, would no doubt be feasting on talk of Sherlock Holmes for the rest of the day. Such it was often with my husband, Dr. John H. Watson, whose boyish hero-worship of his peculiar friend was an unfathomable quirk in an otherwise sane, rational and intelligent character.

But I gave him his head (selflessly, I felt) until shortly after noon, at which time there was a knock at our door. I prayed it would be a patient, but alas, no, and my heart sank at the sight of the traditionally grimy street urchin, bearing a message.

"Holmes is on the case, my dear!" John said, reading the note with excitement. "He wants me to meet him at once in Victoria Station."

"John, really, can't he find his head again without your help?" I protested. But it was too late. He had already dashed into our bedroom to finish dressing, emerging a few minutes later having miraculously shed twenty years from his handsome face. It was suddenly 1890, not 1903, and the mistress of his youth was calling to him once again. With the most perfunctory of kisses he was gone, once more leaving me to conduct my life in solitude.

At times like these I wonder how poor Mary, the first Mrs. John Watson (God rest her soul), dealt with the competition for her husband's attention. How did she cope with the knowledge that her beloved would rather creep through the shadows with his misanthropic ally than spend a quiet evening at home? Speaking for myself I can only say that when John answers the call for adventure and the game is once more afoot, I feel a sense of abandonment greater than I have ever known.

Trying to make the best of it I pulled my favorite book from the shelf (*Little Dorrit*, should anyone care), chose a chapter and began. I had read less than ten pages when there was another knock on the door. "Ma'am," Missy announced, "there is a ragamuffin at the door who says he has a message for the doctor from Mr. Holmes."

Oh, this was too much! I snapped the book closed and marched to the door, where another street Indian, even filthier than the first, stood clutching an envelope. Honestly, so many of these guttersnipes have turned up at our door on behalf of Mr. Sherlock Holmes that I begin to wonder if Fagin is not alive and well and living in upper Baker Street.

After sizing him up and down I said, "Please return to Mr. Holmes at once and tell him that the doctor has already left as a result of his first message, and if that is not fast enough for him, perhaps he should send a coach for him the next time. Now, shoo."

But the boy stood his ground and glared at me with large, luminous, defiant eyes. After a moment he coughed, rather too deliberately, and when that provoked no reaction from me, he held out a dirty hand in a blatant appeal.

"Oh, of course," I said, softening immediately, "something for your trouble. Wait right here." I excused myself, returning a moment later with a fresh bar of soap, which I placed in the urchin's hand. "There you are, now scoot," I commanded, nudging the dumbfounded lad into the hall and closing the door behind him.

I returned to my book and thought no more about the boy or his benefactor until roughly an hour later (three chapters by Dickens time), when the third knock of the afternoon came. I raced Missy to the door, prepared to give the next street Arab. a real piece of my mind to take back to his employer. Imagine my surprise upon finding Sherlock Holmes himself at our humble door.

I had met Holmes only once, at which time we forged a kind of truce regarding my husband's divided affections. But that was before John had nearly been brought up on charges of trespassing in Salisbury, while acting on Holmes' behalf in some exploit that he insists on calling "The Case of the Bishop's Bedchamber." It was therefore with a less than sunny countenance that I greeted the detective, though he hardly noticed. Holmes instead breezed past me and held out a long-fingered hand. "The note if you please," he said, and it took a few self-conscious seconds for me to realize he was talking about the summons he had sent John, which I then retrieved for him.

"As I thought, a clumsy forgery," he said, crumpling the note in his hand.

"Am I to understand that you did not send this?" I asked.

"My message was carried by the lad you so pointedly returned with a cake of lilac bath soap. No, Mrs. Watson, this message is an obvious fraud, and most likely from the same pen as this." He handed over to me another note which read: *Holmes, I must see you. Meet me by the news vendor's at Victoria. Watson.* It looked to me like my husband's handwriting and I said as much.

"Look closely at the pen lines," Holmes said, "and you will notice a series of tiny blots made as the movement of the nib was slowed or stopped altogether. Now examine double e's in the words 'see' and 'meet:' they are perfectly identical, a phenomenon that will never occur naturally in writing."

"What does this mean?" I asked.

"It means the handwriting was traced, letter at a time, or in the case of the identical e's from the same word, from a sample of Watson's own writing."

"Are you in the habit of analysing every such piece of mail you receive, Mr. Holmes?"

"Only the suspicious pieces. This one virtually screamed it's mendacity from across the room."

Foolishly, I asked why.

"Because I know Watson," Holmes replied, "and he would not have asked me to meet him, particularly if the matter were as urgent as the note implies. He would have instead come straight to me."

Like a faithful dog to his master, I thought bitterly, but managed to hold my tongue.

Holmes went on: "I received this note four days ago and immediately saw it for what it truly was: an attempt to lure me into a public place so busy that my abduction would not even be noticed."

"Who on earth would want to abduct you?" I asked, perhaps a bit too brusquely.

"I am not without my enemies, madam, something to

which I'm sure you will attest. But to answer your question directly, I would say it is the same person who has already abducted your husband."

"John!" I cried, sinking down into a chair. "Why would someone want my husband?"

"Oh, he wouldn't," Holmes replied, "except as a means of getting to me. The first attempt to draw me out having failed miserably, our enemy has now taken your husband because he knows I will pursue, following the trail straight into his hands."

Missy appeared dutifully to see if our unexpected guest wished anything, but Holmes waved her away. When she was gone again, I whispered: "How much danger John is in?"

"I fear the worst, madam."

As I tried to collect myself in the wake of this grave pronouncement, Holmes clenched the crumpled note in his hand as though trying to strangle it. "Watson, Watson, why were you taken in by this crude facsimile?" he said.

Because he wanted to be, my mind cried, *because you are able to provide something in his life that I cannot.* But I said none of that, instead asking: "What do we do now?"

"There is very little we can do but wait for the next message." With that the detective took up occupancy in John's chair, steepled his fingers in front of his hawk-like face and closed his eyes. Waiting tries my patience in the best of circumstances, but the sight of Holmes sitting there like a placid, underfed Buddha in this time of crisis nearly made my blood boil. "Shouldn't you be trying to identify the man who kidnapped my husband, instead of taking a nap in my sitting room?" I shouted.

"That is exactly what I am doing, in *here*, " he said, tapping a thin finger to his brow, "where there exists a file of the criminal class more complete than any to be found in Scotland Yard. Now pray, be quiet and allow my mind to work."

How on earth had John put up with this infuriating brute for so many years? My resentment was bubbling to the surface and I was about to give it voice when a more productive thought popped into my head: If the forged notes were, as Holmes claimed, traced directly from handwriting samples, how had those samples been obtained? "His publisher!" I cried, startling Holmes out of his lethargy.

"*Please*, Mrs. Watson... "

"No, listen to me: This mysterious forger had to have samples of John's handwriting to create the note, so where would he get them if not from John's publisher, who has reams of his handwritten manuscripts laying around?"

Holmes eyes snapped open almost audibly and focused on me with the kind of intensity I have not known since my days under the spotlight in the amateur theatre. With catlike grace he leapt out of the chair, complaining that his brain had been "dulled by the disappearance of its whetstone." *That, or a couple decades of cocaine addiction*, I thought.

"I have a manuscript at the publishing house as well," Holmes said, "a monograph that was accepted as a result of your good husband's recommendation. We must go there at once. Come along, Watson!"

I stood still for a moment, stunned by this last command, and I waited for the realization and irony of it to dawn upon him. But it was not forthcoming. Holmes was already out the door, an impatient cry of "Wat-SON!" trailing behind him.

Rushing first to get my hat, I then went down to the street, where Holmes was already waiting for me inside a cab. He performed his best sphinx impersonation for the duration of the cab ride, only coming to life again when we pulled up in front of Neville and Cushing, Publishers, in Theobald's Road.

Mr. Neville, a short round man with duelling plumes of red cheek whiskers, greeted Holmes' arrival as though the King himself had just stepped through the doors. "How grand to see you!" he said, pumping the detective's hand. "Is our dear friend Dr. Watson with you?"

"I'm afraid not, though Mrs. Watson is here," Holmes said, and for the first time Mr. Neville took notice of my existence. "A great pleasure," he declared, halfheartedly, then turned back to Holmes. "We are very anxious to publish your monograph on the art of detection," he said, "I hope you have brought the corrected manuscript with you."

"My dear Mr. Neville, I never took it back," Holmes said.

The round man's face paled. "I don't understand... "

"Pray, tell me everything about the disappearance of my manuscript."

The man was now beginning to perspire. "I would hardly call it a disappearance, Mr. Holmes. It was, after all, your agent who picked it up."

"My agent?"

"The literary agent you share with Dr. Watson; at least that was how he introduced himself. He retrieved both your manuscript and the latest from the doctor, saying that corrections were necessary."

Holmes and I exchanged glances. I knew of no such agent and the expression on Holmes' face indicated the same. "What name did this man go by?" he asked.

"I... I don't remember," the publisher said, now quite flustered.

"Can you at least describe him?"

"Well, I did notice that he possessed a most peculiar skin tone, almost grey. I remember saying that very thing to Mr. ... "

"You have been very helpful, Mr. Neville," Holmes cut in, then spun on his heels and marched briskly out of the shop, shouting "Come along, Watson." I had little choice but to follow.

"Wasn't that a bit rude of you to leave so abruptly?" I said, as Holmes signaled another cab.

"There is little time for pleasantries," he replied. "Besides, the man is ultimately responsible for the theft of my work and that of your husband's, both of which will take considerable time to reproduce. He did, however, provide us with a piece of information that I feel will prove vital."

"Yes, that he is willing to give the store away to anyone who ventures through the door."

Our hansom arrived just then, and once we had stepped inside, Holmes went on. "I was referring to the greyness of this so-called agent's skin, a condition I have observed many times in convicts. Locked up in stone rooms, breathing stale air, denied the privilege of seeing blue sky or green grass, they begin to take on the color of their bleak surroundings."

"So this man is a prisoner?"

"*Was* a prisoner, for he is surely now walking free. But the question remains, why has this man appeared at this very moment in time to launch his plot against me?"

"Perhaps he was just released?"

"And the first thing he does upon his release is plan and perpetrate a serious crime? No, Watson, it won't do."

"*Mrs.* Watson, if you please!"

Ignoring my plea, he went on. "To act thus is the mark of a career criminal, and prison authorities in England are not about to turn a career criminal out onto the streets. No, we must look at the facts."

"Which are...?"

"If our man was not released, he must have escaped, and quite recently, since the greyness of prison walls is still permeating his being. Yet escape from one of London's gaols is virtually an impossible task. Unless... yes, of course, it was right in front of me!"

"And so am I," I reminded him, "therefore I would appreciate being let in on this conversation."

"My apologies," Holmes smirked, meaning none of it. "What would you say if I told you that Newgate prison was slated for demolition this year, necessitating the removal and transfer elsewhere of all remaining inmates?"

"I would say that our man got away during the transfer."

"Bravo, Watson! Our task now is to identify the man in lieu of these facts, for it is much easier to fight an enemy when you know him. I daresay it was someone who went to Newgate as a result of my involvement, since I am the target of the man's revenge. But it is not my life that he wants; that is the interesting point. He could have attempted to kill me any time he wished, but instead he has tried to lure me to him. Why?"

"Perhaps he wants to kill you at home," I said, sweetly.

Holmes ignored the sarcasm. "No, I am convinced the man has something more punishing in mind."

"More punishing than death?"

"You were once in the theatre, were you not? Tell me; who suffers more at the end of *Romeo and Juliet*: the lovers, whose self-inflicted deaths were quick; or their families, who must bear the tragedy they have forged for the rest of their lives?"

I was still pondering this when we arrived at 221b Baker Street. Holmes sprang out of the cab (without bothering to help me down, I might add) and flipped a coin up to the driver.

As often as I had heard about these famous lodgings I had never had cause to visit them. They were a part of John's life (albeit a large part) in which I'd had no involvement. "Why have we come here?" I asked, as we dashed up the staircase.

"I believe I have already identified our mysterious kidnapper," he said, "but I wish to consult the notes I keep regarding all of my cases, to be sure."

He sprinted to his door, rudely leaving me behind, but once there he suddenly froze. "The game progresses more swiftly than I thought," he said. "The next missive is already here."

I must admit that I saw nothing until Holmes pointed to a barely perceptible, grimy hand print on the door jamb. "Here is where the boy leaned when he knelt down to slide a note under the door. He flung open the door and snatched up an envelope that was on the floor, quickly examining it before tearing it open. As he read the note, his face darkened. Without a word he handed it over to me and I recognized the handwriting immediately. *I am well, so far*, it read, *but my host is not a patient man. You are to come at midnight to number 7, Leeside Alley. As you are my friend, Holmes, come alone and unarmed. Watson.*

"The handwriting is quite genuine this time," Holmes said,

"and the address, one of the darkest corners of Limehouse."

"Surely we must go to the police."

Holmes lit a cigarette and burnt away most of it in one long draw. "We cannot bring the police into this. Their bungling would virtually ensure Watson's demise."

"What do we do, then?"

"I will go, of course," Holmes said, releasing a tendril of smoke with each word, "though I'm afraid I cannot honour his wish to go alone."

"But the note says..."

"Mrs. Watson... Amelia... there is so much to do by midnight and so little time. You must trust me."

Whether I truly trusted Sherlock Holmes or not seemed beside the point. He was already formulating his plan — an audacious, if not half-insane one — and the ally he planned to take with him into the mouth of danger was *me*. But if it meant that John would be brought back to safety, I was willing.

* * *

We approached three cabs before finding a driver willing to take us into the heart of Limehouse Hole at midnight.

Number 7 Leeside Alley turned out be a black, ominous looking house; if Mephistopheles had wished to place the rear entrance to Hell somewhere in England, he could not have done better. A nearby church tower told us it was the appointed time. "Take courage," Holmes whispered to me as we approached the door, which opened without our having to knock.

A hard looking man stood in the doorway. "I was told t'expect just one o' you," he growled, "oo's this."

"Amelia Watson, wife of the doctor," Holmes said for me, "now let us in." He literally pushed his way inside, with myself following on unsteady legs, and demanded that we be taken to see my husband.

We were led down a dark, tunnel-like hallway to a small door which opened into a dank, odorous cellar. Proceeding down the creaky stair was difficult, particularly for me, but we finally made it to the bottom, where a heart-wrenching sight nearly caused me to swoon.

In the dim illumination of one lantern I could see John bound tightly to a chair, gagged, blindfolded and helpless. I nearly cried out but Holmes stopped me by appearing to stumble in the darkness and fell against me, using this diversion to whisper into my ear: "Remember, say nothing; let me do the talking." I forced myself to remain strong, as Holmes announced, "I am here, as you demanded."

From the shadows, a voice said: "I told you to come alone," and Holmes once again explained who I was, adding (truthfully) that I was nearly distraught with fear for the safety of my husband.

"I see," the voice said, "a witness might not be a bad idea after all. Have you at least honoured my command to come unarmed?"

"I have," Holmes answered, "on that you have my word."

"Ah, yes, the word of Sherlock Holmes, upon which so much relies." Up to this point we had simply been shadows talking to another shadow, but now the criminal walked into the circle of light where he could be seen. His face was that of Sherlock Holmes!

The real Holmes drowned out any sounds of my surprise by saying: "An excellent likeness, Stephens, but then it would be, having been taken from my effigy at Madame Tussaud's."

A startled gasp came from under the mask, which the man ripped off a moment later. The publisher's description had been all too apt: the gaunt man was indeed a sickly shade of grey. "How did you...?" he sputtered.

"Deduce that you were James Stephens, late of Newgate Prison, recently escaped, though presumed dead?" Holmes said. "You all but gave it away in the note you so obviously dictated to the good Watson: *My host is an impatient man.* Your impatience led to carelessness seventeen years ago when you tried to rob Drummond's Bank. That was as much responsible for your capture as I was."

Gnashing his teeth, the grey man spat, "But it was your testimony that sent me to my fate."

"I simply told the truth."

"Yes, and the truth is all important to you, isn't it, Holmes? Do you remember at the dock, before they took me away, how I swore vengeance against you?"

"As I recall, you claimed that someday, somehow, you would destroy me."

"And I will, completely, utterly and without mercy!" Stephens then pulled out a razor and held it dangerously close to John's throat! I gasped, but a cough from Holmes told me to control my emotions for a little while longer.

"Seventeen years of my life have been wasted in a cell," Stephens said, "but I plan to make up for that loss by dying a rich man. A very rich man. I am planning a crime spree that will make anything perpetrated by that pompous fool Moriarty pale by comparison! And you, Mr. Holmes, will sit back and watch, completely unable to stop me."

"Prison has unhinged you, I fear," the detective said.

"You are wrong. It has made me see my true destiny more clearly. Owen... " he commanded, and the man who answered the door handed him some sort of document. "The world is black and white to you, isn't it, Holmes? No gradations, no justifications, just black or white, honorable or dishonourable, good or evil, simple as that. Am I right?"

"It is not quite so simple as that," Holmes replied, "though I admit that there are certain matters in which no compromise is possible."

"You are a prig!" Stephens suddenly shouted, "a prig whose melodramatic, schoolboy sense of right and wrong has ruined countless lives!"

"Those that deserved to be ruined."

"Like mine, I suppose?" The man's eyes had turned into black holes consumed by hate, and there was little doubt in my mind we were dealing with a lunatic. "What would you do to save the life of your friend, Holmes?" the man went on. "What would you sacrifice? Your career, perhaps? Your reputation?"

"You grow tiresome, Stephens," Holmes sighed, "play your hand and be done with it."

The criminal smiled victoriously as he thrust the paper towards us. "This document, which is in your handwriting, courtesy of our steady-handed friend Mr. Owen, is nothing less than your sworn statement that you will never make any attempt to stop or hinder me, or any of my confederates. Dr. Watson will be released once you have signed your name at the bottom — in *blood*."

I could feel Holmes tense beside me.

"It is a moral dilemma, is it not, Holmes?" Stephens went on. "If you sign, you are honour bound to relinquish all activity and watch helplessly while I take over the city of London. If you do not sign, your friend and colleague is murdered before your very eyes."

"What makes you think I would honour this ridiculous forgery, even if I did sign it?"

"You disappoint me, Holmes. I would have thought the word of the great, self-righteous Sherlock Holmes would be enough to hold you. But since you seem to require more incentive, think about Watson: what do you suppose his life would be worth should you ever break your word and try to fight me?"

The stillness that descended upon the dark, squalid room at that moment was like a vacuum. "I said I would destroy you, Holmes," Stephens finally resumed, "and I will, piece by piece, each time I commit a new crime that you are honour-bound to ignore. Unless, of course, Watson is not worth that price."

"*Stop*," Holmes moaned in a voice steeped in defeat, "you know that he is. Mrs. Watson, there is a pin in your hat, I believe?"

Holmes himself withdrew the pin and stabbed the finger, which was now poised over the diabolical document. But before any blood touched the paper, he said: "First release Watson."

The horrible Stephens smiled and bowed graciously. Then taking the razor he carelessly hacked through John's bonds until my husband fell to the floor. I started towards him but Holmes held me back.

"Now, sign!" the villain demanded.

I had never before seen a signature written in blood, and it was not an easy task. But soon the name *Sherlock Holmes* was on the document. As the criminal snatched it away I tucked my hand into my pocket, knowing the moment had now come.

Stephens examined the paper gleefully, but after a few seconds his face paled even further. "This is not the signature of Sherlock Holmes!" he cried. I then grasped the revolver in my pocket, a task made quite painful because of my sore, bleeding finger — for it was I dressed in the top hat and long coat, teetering on four inch wedges inside overly-large boots, with my face buried under paint and putty that had been molded into the visage of Sherlock Holmes!

"Now, Watson!" Holmes cried, and I tossed the gun, which he deftly caught with a gloved hand. "The game is up, Stephens," he said, ripping off the veil and wig that contributed to his disguise as Amelia Watson!

"You tricked me!" Stephens screamed. Still grasping the razor, he lunged for the prone figure of my husband. But with a deafening *crack* Holmes fired the revolver, sending a bullet through the villain's shoulder, and with a great cry he collapsed on the floor, next to John. Lurching towards him as fast as my boots would allow, I kicked the razor out of his hand and sent it skittering into a corner. But then out of the darkness came a second shadow, this one bearing an iron poker. "Holmes, behind you!" I cried, and the detective spun around in time to dodge a murderous blow. He fired off another shot, striking Owen in the leg and felling him.

As Holmes secured the moaning villains, I ministered to John, releasing the gag from his mouth and the blindfold from his eyes. "It is I, my darling," I said, and kissed him passionately, but when I withdrew I saw that he had fainted dead away. Only then did I remember that I was still wearing the face of Sherlock Holmes!

Michael Mallory

* * *

John slept for most of the next day, but by late afternoon he was up and eager to learn the details of his rescue. I forced him to wait until Holmes' arrival, which occurred shortly before tea.

"As soon as I read of the missing head from the wax museum," Holmes began, "I suspected that you were in danger, Watson. Why else would someone steal a replica of my head unless to create a mask from it, and why would someone do that if not to convince a third party that he was me."

"It *was* convincing from a distance," John confirmed, "but as soon as I got close I realized the deception. But by then it was too late, the blackguards had a gun trained on me. But really, Holmes, I don't know if I shall ever forgive you for subjecting my wife to such danger."

"And I would not have done so, old friend, if I were not convinced that she would be able to handle herself, which, I need not tell you, she did admirably."

John stroked my face, now cleansed of Holmes' makeup, and gazed lovingly at me. Dear, sweet, loving John.

Holmes went on: "Once we were able to identify of our enemy I recalled his courtroom oath and deduced that the purpose of this dangerous game was to extract from me some concession that would otherwise have been repugnant to me, using nothing less than your life as collateral on the agreement. The problem then became how to fight such a plot, for Stephens was correct in one regard: my word *is* inviolable, even when given to a creature such as him. An obvious solution presented itself: An impostor in the place of Sherlock Holmes could agree to anything. So I turned Stephens' own trick back on him. I counted on the fact that it would be dark, which would aid the deception, and used simple stage ventriloquism to speak through your wife. Though I did not foresee the painful business of the blood signature, and for that I am truly sorry."

Holmes nervously touched my arm, which was probably as close to a pat of apology and concern as one could ever hope to receive from him.

"But I heard you give your word that you were unarmed," John was saying.

"And so I was. It was your wife who carried the gun."

John glared at me reproachfully. "Oh, don't give me that look," I laughed, "not after all the times I have chastised you for playing with firearms."

Holmes tried unsuccessfully to stifle a snort of amusement at this admonishment — as though he were guiltless.

"Answer this then, Holmes," John continued, somewhat humbled, "why Amelia? Why couldn't someone else have stood in for you?"

"A fair question," the detective said. "There were three reasons: first, there was no time to secure the services of another, we had to proceed immediately. Second, I knew she was trained as an actress. And the third I should think is quite obvious: Surely you have noticed that your wife and I share the same facial features; even without makeup we are nearly identical."

At this pronouncement my mouth flew open and I saw John's do the same. I certainly saw no resemblance, and I doubt my husband did, though I must confess that the complexities inherent in that statement have kept me awake more than one night since this adventure took place.

But if Holmes noticed our startled expressions he did not show it. Instead he got up and started to leave, but at the door he turned back and smiled at John. "Over the years you have heard me speak time and again of *the* woman," he said. "I hope you will not think me untoward if I tell you that I believe I have met *the other* woman. Take care of her, Watson."

With that, Mr. Sherlock Holmes made his way out of our home, if not our lives.

THE ADVENTURE OF THE RIPPER'S SCRAWL

"John, I wish to leave immediately," I said quietly but firmly.

"But my dear, we have only just arrived," my husband replied.

"We have been at this dreadful party exactly fifty-three minutes, which has nothing to do with my wanting to leave."

John smiled at another passing chorus of stuffed shirts with champagne glasses, then asked: "Are you unwell?" This is invariably the first question from his lips whenever I bespeak a complaint of any kind — presumably the effect of so many years as a medical man.

"Physically, I have never been better, but I refuse to stay in the same room with that horrible man over there. The brute made overtures towards me!"

"The damnable cad! Which one is he?"

I levelled an accusatory finger at the villain, but upon spotting him the fiery indignation that had flared in John's eyes quickly cooled. "Amelia, that is Lord Wilby, undersecretary for home affairs," he groaned.

"Who is now trying to negotiate an affair of his own," I snapped back. "I demand you defend my honour."

"My dear, one cannot go about assailing a member of the government like Don Quixote charging the windmill."

While normally the most considerate of men, there are still odd moments when John can be as infuriating as his misanthropic friend, Sherlock Holmes. I was about to tell him so when our host suddenly appeared. "Is something the matter, Mrs. Watson? You look distressed," said Sir Melville Macnaghten.

"It is nothing," John replied before I could get a word

out, "my wife just remembered she... forgot to wind the clock. Isn't that right, dear?"

"If you say so, darling," I said coolly, while throwing him a glare that screamed: *We will speak more of this later.*

"I see," our host said, obviously not convinced but polite enough to let the matter drop. Like John, Sir Melville Macnaghten was sturdily built and wore a moustache, though he was considerably shorter and nowhere near as handsome. The sum of my knowledge regarding him was that he was a career police official who had called upon John for professional assistance in the past, and who had just been appointed head of Scotland Yard's Criminal Investigation Department. This evening's *soiree* at his home in Chelsea was to celebrate the promotion.

"I'm very pleased you could come this evening," Sir Melville was saying. "I also invited your friend Holmes, though I did not receive a reply."

"Mr. Holmes is not much of one for dinner parties," I said, leaving unspoken the thought that in this instance, I did not blame him.

"Oh, it is nothing so simple as that, Mrs. Watson," Sir Melville said. "Holmes has not spoken to me for twelve years."

"Heavens, what did you do to him?"

A tiny smile broke out under his moustache. "I had the temerity to solve the Ripper case."

"Jack the Ripper?" I said, "I thought that still unsolved."

"Officially, it still is, due to the Vurczak business."

I was now completely lost. "Werjack? What is a werjack?"

"Not what, Mrs. Watson, who. Vurczak was an immigrant butcher living in the East End, who for a time was the Yard's leading suspect. He was later exonerated, but not before a neighbourhood mob, believing him to be the Ripper, hunted him down and killed him."

"How awful," I said.

"Yes, it was unsettling, to say the least," Sir Melville acknowledged. "But because of that incident I have never made public my case against the man I believe to be Jack the Ripper. Even though the man himself is now dead, his family remains vulnerable."

"Sir Melville did, however, disclose his theory to Holmes and me," John said, "though Holmes took exception with his conclusions."

"Quite strongly," Sir Melville added. "In the end he declared that the next time he spoke to me it would be to provide the Ripper's true identity, and since he has never come up with a suspect of his own he has not spoken to me since 1891."

"He still remains convinced, though, that there is a secret message hidden inside that scrawl," John said.

"What scrawl?" I asked, not because I particularly wanted to know, but because I hated being left out of a conversation.

"The Ripper left a message in chalk on a wall near two of the murder sites," Sir Melville answered. "It read, *The Juwes are not the men that will be blamed for nothing.*"

"What on earth does that mean?"

"No one knows. Equally puzzling was the fact that the word *Jews* was spelled J-U-W-E-S, which I'm told has Masonic significance."

Given the ghastly direction this conversation had taken, I was not unhappy when it was interrupted by the sudden appearance in the room of a uniformed constable, who marched straight to Sir Melville and began whispering in his ear. I saw Sir Melville's face darken and when the constable had finished he turned to me, taking my hand. "Mrs. Watson, I am terribly sorry, but I need to borrow your husband. I am afraid we must leave at once."

"What has happened?" John asked, and for an instant I saw the lightning flash of youthful excitement that comes over him whenever he is summoned by Holmes.

"I cannot explain now, but your medical expertise shall be of great use to me, doctor. Mrs. Watson, would you be so good as to give my regrets to the rest of the guests? Say I was called away on official business."

I started to protest, but Sir Melville cut me off with a clipped, "Thank you," and marched out of the room, taking my husband with him.

***

It was nearly two o'clock when John returned home. I was still awake, having been restlessly wandering through the pages of *Little Dorrit.* I had every intention of berating him for abandoning at the party and forcing me to find my own way home. However, one look at him caused my anger to abate. Pale, exhausted and shaking, John had obviously had a much worse night than I. "Would you mind telling me what that was all about?" was the best I could do.

"Murder, my dear," John said softly. "A man's body was found in an alleyway near Soho."

"Dear God!"

"Oh, that's only the beginning. I knew the man. At least I

knew him years ago when we he was a young medical student. Thedgehughes was his name. He was quite a brilliant student, but then something happened to him and he seemed to drop completely out of sight. I hadn't seen him since his training days at Bart's. Until tonight."

"I'm so sorry, darling."

"I haven't told you the worst yet, Amelia. The body had been... *ripped*. And on a nearby wall someone had written the scrawl."

"The scrawl? John, you can't mean —"

"It was exactly the same as Sir Melville quoted, misspelt word for word."

"What does it mean?"

John looked at me with eyes reddened by fear and exhaustion. "It means we brought him back, Amelia. Somehow, with all our talk of the Whitechappel murders last evening, we managed to resurrect Jack the Ripper."

***

The next day's newspapers featured a full account of the horrible murder, including the fact that it was John who identified the body, yet the papers stopped short of linking the murder to Jack the Ripper. That would not happen for another week, when the body of a wealthy silk merchant, improbably named Galahad Arnaught, turned up near the docks. Hastily written across the pavement near the body was the scrawl. Still clinging to the irrational fear that he was somehow responsible, this second horror seemed to bother John even more than the first. But it was the third such killing, which was reported three days later, that seemed to cast him into a near total state of despondency.

"The blood-drenched body of Sir Robert Blamefort was discovered in the early morning hours, near Seven Dials. His throat had been slashed, his abdomen..."

"John, must you read that aloud?" I protested.

"Sorry," he muttered, dropping the paper down on the floor next to his chair. Then with sudden and startling agitation, he cried: "When will this terrible business end? What is the meaning of it all? Why are men of status being struck down instead of women of the streets?"

"John, you cannot seriously be arguing that the lives of the male aristocracy are worth more than women of the common classes."

"No, no, no, of course not, it's just that..." he stopped for a moment, struggling to find the right words, "... it is part of a pattern, Amelia, it has to be; the choice of seemingly unrelated victims, that damnable scrawl, it all adds up to *something*. But what am I doing to help discover the answer? *Nothing*! Why on earth hasn't Holmes contacted me?"

At long last I realized the source of John's dark mood. A major crime spree was taking place, a puzzle of immense proportions, and he was being left out of the investigation.

Up to this point I had been secretly rejoicing the silence coming from Baker Street, knowing that every time John returned to Holmes I was all but forgotten. On the other hand, a few lonely nights would still be preferable to watching him brood so. After carefully weighing the consequences, I suggested: "Why don't you go to Mr. Holmes and find out?"

"Yes, yes, perhaps I should," John said, "I shall go at once." He readied himself quickly, kissed me goodbye and left.

I asked our maid Missy to put off her afternoon duties for a leisurely game of chess — something that required very little persuasion — but much to my surprise John was back in less than an hour, looking like he had witnessed the execution of his best friend.

"Now what is it?" I asked. "Was Mr. Holmes gone?"

"Oh, no, he was there," John said quietly while staring at the floor. "He turned me away."

"The brute!"

"But he sent a message."

"A message?"

"Yes, it seems he did not want to see me at all," John said, sounding like a hurt child, "he wants to see you, Amelia."

***

I was ushered up to the hallowed rooms of 221b by Martha Hudson, Holmes' chatty, grey-haired landlady. "He's in one of his moods, dear," she whispered conspiratorially as we approached the door. I knocked and received the barked reply: "Come in, Mrs. Watson!"

My first thought upon entering was to race back out to tell Mrs. Hudson that her house was on fire, so thick was the smoke. But it turned out to be nothing more than the product of Holmes overworked pipe. "Could we please open a window?" I coughed.

"As you wish," Holmes said impatiently, throwing open the window and letting some of the noxious cloud escape into Baker Street.

"Thank you. Now, Mr. Holmes, before I say anything else I must tell you that I do not appreciate your latest cavalier dismissal of John. He was positively crushed."

"Watson knows me better than anyone, madam, he will get over it. But come, look at this." He forcefully directed my attention through the smoky haze to a chalkboard on which was written the scrawl of the Ripper, now horribly familiar.

"*This* is why you asked me up here?" I said. "I would have thought that you would be out investigating these horrible murders instead of practising your handwriting."

Holmes luminous grey eyes pierced the acrid smoke like the fog lights of a coach. "The police, it seems, have chosen not to invite me into their investigations, and there is very little a consulting detective can do if no one elects to consult him."

At that instant I felt a touch of sympathy for him. Like John, he had been completely left out in the cold. No, that was not quite right: John had been involved in the discovery of the first victim. What a blow to Holmes' ego it must have been to read in the papers that his Boswell had been asked to assist in a murder case whereas he had not. That at least could explain the curt dismissal of his old friend.

"But that is of little consequence," Holmes said, waving his hand, "since I am convinced that this scrawl holds the answer to both sets of murders."

"I still do not see what this has to do with me."

Much to my dismay he refilled his pipe from a filthy-looking old slipper and lit it, sending another gust of thick blue smoke into the room. "I am now convinced that the person who wrote this scrawl was a man of the theatre, and that the key which will unlock its message is a deep knowledge of the works of Shakespeare — a deeper knowledge than even I myself possess, which is why I have called upon you. As a former actress you surely have more than a passing acquaintance with the Bard."

I stared at him in wonderment. "Well, yes, but what could possibly lead you to see a Shakespearean connection?"

"I will show you." He pointed to the chalkboard. "As written, the message is meaningless, agreed?" Without waiting for my reply he rubbed out the last two words, *for nothing*, and asked, "Now, what about this?" I had to admit that what was left made a complete, grammatically correct thought: *The Juwes are not the men who will be blamed.* Then I saw what he had obviously wanted me to see. "It is written in iambic pentameter."

"Precisely."

"But can you really afford to discard the last two words?"

"Yes, because they are *for nothing*," he said. "Now then, because of it's spelling the word *Juwes* stands out, so let us start with it. The most famous Jew in Shakespeare is, of course..." He finished the sentence by writing out the word *Shylock* on the board. "You see, I am not totally ignorant of the Swan of Avon. But note that the word is plural. Therefore I ask you what other Shakespearean characters fall into that category?"

Goodness, how many years had it been since I had performed the classics with the Delancey Amateur Players? More than I cared to disclose. I tried to think back to our little group, conjuring up the faces of the other actors in the company and matching them with the roles they played. After a minute it came to me. "There another Jewish character in *Merchant of Venice*, named *Tubal*," I told him.

"Tubal," Holmes repeated, jotting the word down on the board. Then his eyes lit up. "I believe you have scored a hit on the first attempt!" After the word *Tubal* he wrote *Cain*. "Tubal-Cain is the secret password of the Freemasons," he said, excitedly, "which explains the Masonic spelling of the word *Jews*. Therefore, the answer to this devious equation would appear to be the word *cain*. Now, where does that lead us? The Biblical Cain, perhaps? The first murderer, slayer of his own brother? "

"Brother against brother," I mused, "perhaps a reference to civil war?"

Holmes considered this. "An interesting thought, and one that points towards an American, since wars in Europe are generally fought country to country, not brother to brother. But let us translate it back into our theme; where do we find war, brotherly or otherwise, in the works of Shakespeare?"

"*Henry the Fifth* is set against the war between England and France."

"You are invaluable, Watson."

"*Mrs.* Watson, if you please. And my knowledge of the *Henry* comes from the fact that I understudied the role of Katherine once and had a terrible time with the language. It is partly written in French."

He spun around and faced the chalkboard. "Partly written in French... of course! How could I have been so stupid!" As I looked on, perplexed, he circled the word *men* and then stepped back to look at the board. Just then our attention was drawn to a loud coughing coming from the door. Waving her way through the haze, and spluttering mightily, was Mrs. Hudson.

"Ooh, really, Mr. Holmes!" she cried, "I have put up with your habits for a goodly number of years, but I'll be blamed if I will let this continue! My kitchen is full of smoke!"

"My abject apologies, Mrs. Hudson, but at the moment we are — " Holmes stopped dead and then a rare beaming smile broke out on his face. "Mrs. Hudson, you are a jewel!" he cried. Then throwing an arm around her shoulder, he began walking her back towards the door. "I will make every effort to change my living habits, but for now I must ask you to go back to your kitchen, smoke filled though it may be, while Mrs. Watson and I continue to work, and thank you so much." With a gentle nudge he pushed her through the door and closed it behind her.

As I watched, puzzled, Holmes raced back to the board, the circled *be blamed*. "An English colloquialism, usually used in place of *be damned*, particularly by elderly landladies," he said, a grin dancing over his lips. "And this..." he tapped the chalk on the circled word *men*, "translated into French becomes *hommes*. Which gives us... "

I watched, half in awe, half in disbelief, as he decoded the circled words and came up with: SHYLOCK HOMMES BE DAMNED. "As I have long suspected," he said, "this scrawl was a personal taunt directed at me by the most fiendish killer London has ever known."

In different circumstances I would have accredited Holmes discovery of the message to coincidence, fuelled by megalomania. But in the potent, smoky atmosphere of his rooms, I was swayed. In addition, I could see yet another clue in the words that were left. "Mr. Holmes, if you put the *t* from *not* after the *a* in are, and you get — "

"*Theatre*," he finished, writing it on the board. "And *will*, for Will Shakespeare, no doubt. This leaves us *o*, *n*, *w* and *h*. What do you make of that?"

My head was throbbing. "Well, *w*, *h* and *o* spell *who*."

"Which is the information we seek — *who*? The last remaining letter, *n*, is obviously the answer. It is most likely an initial."

"Whose initial, Mr. Holmes?"

"I should say it is a person trained in the classical theatre, probably an actor, perhaps an American, though with knowledge of French and English colloquialisms, and a man with contempt for the police, for why else would he direct his message to me instead of the Yard? But to answer your question directly, Mrs. Watson, "*N* is initial of Jack the Ripper."

* * *

"John, please answer honestly," I said at supper the next

evening, "has Mr. Holmes ever been so stunningly and brilliantly wrong that his conclusions, while impressive at first, later appear laughable?"

"Why do you ask?" John said glumly. He was still his sulk.

"I keep thinking of the way he pulled words and meaning out of that scrawl. It rather reminded me of a fellow I once knew who was convinced that someone else had really written the works of Shakespeare and was forever twisting around the text and pulling out hidden clues that were not really there to support his theory."

At this point Missy reappeared to clear our plates and bring John his evening *Times* (his reading at the table is a habit I fear I shall never be able to break him of). Once she had gone, I continued: "What if Mr. Holmes were guilty of the same thing? What if, after so many years of searching, he wanted to find a message to badly that... John, are you listening?"

My husband's face had gone pale as he stared at the newspaper. Finally he read: "Early this morning police discovered the fourth victim of a killer being called the modern-day Jack the Ripper. The body of Mr. Francis Notting, a solicitor, was found behind his house in Stoke Newington."

Despite the warming fire in the hearth I felt cold. *Notting* began with an *N*, the initial identified by Holmes as being the Ripper's. Yet this Notting had been one of the victims, not the killer.

Just then a thought struck me and I gasped, so loudly that John was startled. "Amelia, are you all right?" he asked.

My voice quavered as I said, "We must see Mr. Holmes immediately."

"Whatever for?"

"I have just realized the meaning of the Ripper's scrawl."

***

"You must think me a complete fool, Mrs. Watson," Sherlock Holmes muttered as he studied the changes I had made to the scrawl.

"Nonsense," I said, taking care not to further abrade his ego, "I am sure you would have discovered it too, at some point." Still, it was with some pride that I glanced back at the dusty chalkboard, which had been erased and written more than a hundred times, and upon which was now printed:

THEDGEHUGHES ARNAUGHT
THE MEN THAT WILL BE

BLAMEFORT NOTTING.

"My congratulations, Mrs. Watson," Holmes was saying, "though someone has obviously beaten both of us to the solution."

John, meanwhile, was muttering: "*Four* men worked together to commit the Ripper killings; it is unbelievable."

"On the contrary, Watson," Holmes said, "it fits only too well. Consider the letters and postcards sent to the police and the newspapers from Jack the Ripper, each in a different handwriting; the conflicting descriptions of suspects from eyewitnesses; the reason Saucy Jack was so absurdly successful in eluding the entire Metropolitan police force — one man took the chance of being caught only once, and if he subsequently became a suspect I daresay he would have had an unbreakable alibi for each of the other murders. It was a conspiracy as clever as it was diabolical, and one which is now about to play its final act."

"Final act?"

"Think Watson! There were *five* Ripper murders, not four, therefore one name remains inside the scrawl."

John scanned the blackboard. "I see no other names."

"Watson, Watson," Holmes cried, "you see but you do not observe!" And in this instance I regretfully had to agree with him. Taking up the chalk, Holmes circled the words *will be.*

"Holmes, you can't mean —"

"Yes, Watson, the name of the fifth Ripper is *Wilby* — which can only mean Lord Wilby."

"For heaven's sake, Holmes, the man is a member of government! Surely there are other men named Wilby."

"Yes, but none with enough power and influence to cover up such an unholy conspiracy for so long. If we could only get to him in time we might be able to intercept the killer before he exacts his final revenge," Holmes said.

"Revenge?"

"Yes, Watson, that is what this case is about, revenge. I was stupid not to realize it before." Holmes was now in such a stage of nervous agitation that he appeared to emit smoke without the benefit of his pipe. "But how can we get to Wilby when we don't even know where he lives?"

I suddenly remembered something I had spent a fortnight trying to block out. "I have his address, Mr. Holmes!" I shouted, digging through my handbag until I found the calling card. "He slipped it to me at Sir Melville's party. I told you the man was a beast, John."

"There is not a moment to lose!" Holmes cried, snatching

the card out of my hand and slipping it into his vest pocket. Into his coat pocket he secreted a small revolver. "Come along, Watson!"

"I am coming, too," I said.

"Absolutely not!" John commanded.

"John, hear me out: by now Lord Wilby must know that he is to be the next victim. Do you think he is going to open his door to just anyone? As much as it disgusts me to contemplate, he *did* invite me to his home."

"She is right, Watson," Holmes said, "your wife may be our only way in. Now, come!"

John and Holmes flew down the flight of stairs to the street as though they had done it a thousand times before, which indeed, they must have, while I struggled with my skirt every step of the way. Outside Holmes was already hailing a cab. After offering the driver an extra half-crown if he could get us to Wilby's Mayfair address within ten minutes, we piled in for a coach ride the likes of which I had never experienced, and with luck, never shall again. We raced through the night like entrants in a steeplechase, bouncing over every cobble and brick in the streets, rounding every corner at such a speed that I felt we would surely tip over. To his credit the driver managed to keep the brougham upright while earning his bonus, though by the time we reached Lord Wilby's home I felt like little pieces of my being had been shaken off and left behind.

Leaping from the coach, Holmes raced to Lord Wilby's door and began pounding on it. "I fear we may be too late," he said, thumping more and more violently. Finally he cried: "Come, Watson, we must break it in!" and the two of them began throwing their combined weight against the door.

"John, be careful of your shoulder!" I called out, knowing he would be in agony the next morning. But he was on a case and nothing else mattered. When the bolt finally gave way Holmes and John rushed in to find a servant lying on the floor, a heavy bruise discolouring his forehead. With obvious effort the man then opened his eyes and whispered: "Upstairs... the study."

"Quickly, then!" Holmes shouted, pulling the revolver from his pocket and dashing up the wide staircase with John in pursuit. Lifting up my skirts almost above my knees, I dashed as well.

Voices were coming from behind one of the upstairs panelled doors, which Holmes burst through, pistol in hand, closely followed by John. As I rushed in behind them, I could see Lord Wilby trapped in an overstuffed chair by a large brutish man dressed in a leather butcher's apron. One of the man's huge hands grasped

Wilby's shoulder, holding him down, while the other held a knife to his throat.

"Do not make a move!" Holmes commanded, and in a heavily-accented voice the man growled back, "This no concern of yours!"

"Murder is always a concern of mine, Vurczak."

"Vurczak?" I blurted out, "I thought he was dead."

The man with the knife turned to look at me and I realized that, brutish or not, he was far too young to have been a suspect in the Ripper murders. Then the truth struck me. "Vurczak the butcher was your father, wasn't he?"

The fierce scowl on his face faded away, revealing underneath the look of a lost little boy. "I was six year old when they kill Papa," he said. "He was good man, and they kill him because this pig and his friends cut up those whores!" The knife scraped Wilby's neck. "Tell them!" the man shouted.

"All right," Wilby gasped. "It's true... there were five of us who killed the prostitutes... now let me go."

But instead of letting him go Vurczak pressed the knife even closer until a thin trickle of red ran down Lord Wilby's neck. At that instant the sound of a gunshot echoed through the room, startling everyone except Holmes. "The next time, I shall not miss," he said, "now drop the knife!"

Throwing us a look of sheer hatred, the butcher lowered his arm and let the knife fall to the floor, then let loose of Wilby.

"That's better," Holmes said. "Now, Lord Wilby, the truth."

"The truth, Mr. Holmes? It *is* Holmes, is it not? Of course it is; who else would it be?" Wilby took out a handkerchief and pressed it to his neck. "I have already been forced to admit a great deal, and I doubt telling you the rest can hurt me. After all, there is nothing you will be able to do about it. But before you rush to judgement, bear in mind how young we were then and how easy it was for young, affluent gentlemen to become bored. You see, there was nothing we could not afford, nothing we had not tried. Nothing except murder."

I felt my blood chilling and reached out to John for warmth and support.

"We formed a little club, the five of us, the most exclusive club in London," Wilby went on. "We chose the East End to do our work for obvious reasons. It was already overpopulated by the expendables of society: the poor, the diseased, the criminal classes, immigrants. Of them all, prostitutes were the obvious victims."

"Why, because they were women?" I demanded angrily.

"Because they were women who were used to being approached by strange men," he sneered, "women who conducted their vile business in the shadows, unseen, the same way we needed to conduct our business. You know, when all is said and done, we were helping rid society of a scourge."

"Even if that were true, it hardly explains the mutilation of the victims," Holmes said.

"Oh, that. As part of the club initiation, proof was required that the deed had been done, and what could be more conclusive than a piece of the victim herself?" Had I been armed at that moment I might have tried to kill the man myself.

"But then something unexpected happened," he continued. "Jack the Ripper — my appellation, by the way — started to develop a life of his own. Before long the game had changed; it was no longer simply about the thrill of murder. Now it was about notoriety and danger and trying to outdo one another in brutality and audacity. We started writing to the police, taunting them, almost daring them to catch us. We even began leaving clues to our identities such as that message that Blamefort left on the wall, which he thought was so clever. That business of misspelling the word *Jews* was his revenge against the Freemasons, who had expelled him for some reason or other. He wanted them implicated, you see. At any rate, we knew the message would never be deciphered."

"Yet it was," Holmes said.

"But not by this lout," Wilby said, gesturing contemptuously towards Vurczak, "I doubt that he can even read. It was Thedgehughes who tipped the pot. He was always the weakest amongst us. I think it is fair to say that the knowledge of what he had done haunted him, and ultimately ruined him. In a drunken stupor one night it seems he blurted out the entire story to a stranger in a tavern, not realizing that he was confessing to his executioner."

"He tell me everything," Vurczak said. "I kill him for it. Then I find the others and kill them, too, these dogs that let my papa die for their sins!"

"Yes, yes, yes," Wilby said, impatiently. "The ultimate irony, of course, is that our club was dissolved because of this oaf's sire. When he was killed by the mob I realized that we had far more to fear from the outraged public than the police. We decided to retire Jack, though I suspect a couple of the lads continued on their own over the years." Wilby reached into his coat for a cigar and with unbearable casualness, said: "I trust no one minds if I smoke?"

"I for one wouldn't mind if you burned," I replied.

Regarding me with annoyance, he muttered: "What a mistake it was to give you my card. I should have realized immediately you were not the type."

"Nor am I the type to attend murder trials," I shot back, trying to control my voice, "though I think I shall enjoy seeing you in the dock."

"Oh, don't be stupid, madam," he sneered, lighting his cigar. "Nothing will happen to me. I am too important to His Majesty's government. *There* is your killer, Holmes, take him and get him out of here."

"Take the gun, Watson," Holmes said, "and keep it pointed it straight at Vurczak's heart. If he makes a move of any kind, shoot him."

Though obviously puzzled, John complied. Holmes went on: "I caution you to remain still, Vurczak, for Dr. Watson is an excellent shot. And as for you, Lord Wilby, I have no doubt that what you say is true. You would never be prosecuted for these crimes."

"It is such a rare pleasure to deal with an intelligent man," Wilby said. "I will see Macnaghten in the morning about charges against this fellow. Now please leave, all of you."

"As you wish," Holmes said. "You can put the gun away now, Watson, our business here is finished. We are leaving." He turned and started towards the door.

The blasé veneer suddenly fell away from his Lordship. "What are you talking about?" he cried, "you are taking this villain with you!"

"I think not," said Holmes.

"But he is a murderer!"

"As are you, my lord, and all murderers must come to justice one way or other. I assure you I will do everything in my power to see that this man is apprehended."

"Holmes, you cannot walk out of here and leave me defenceless!"

"Of course not," Holmes replied, reaching into the pocket of his trousers and pulling out a jackknife, which he opened and flung down on the floor. "Defend yourself with that."

As soon as we were out of the study Holmes slammed the door shut. From inside the room we heard the sounds of a struggle followed by a scream. Then the screaming stopped. "What a pity we were too late," Holmes said quietly.

* * *

For the next week the newspapers did little except decry the horrible tragedy and publish tribute after tribute to the late Lord Rodger Wilby. I could read none of them.

Even though Wilby's servant and Holmes both offered the police a description of Vurczak the police were unable to find any trace of him. "I doubt he will be seen again," Mr. Holmes said as he peered out the window of his Baker Street den, into which Mrs. Hudson was bringing a pot of piping hot tea and a tray of cakes. "He is most likely on board a ship headed for parts unknown by now."

"Will the truth ever be made public?" I asked.

"Perhaps someday," he said, then reached for his top hat and walking stick. "I must leave you now."

"Where on earth are you off to?" John asked, helping himself to a tea cake.

"I have an appointment with Sir Melville Macnaghten," Holmes said, flashing one of those electric, quicksilver smiles. "I am sure Mrs. Hudson will permit you to stay as long as you like. Goodbye." He then dashed out of the rooms like the White Rabbit.

As John happily chatted with his former landlady, I scanned the cluttered rooms he used to call home. Invariably my gaze returned to the chalkboard, on which the horrid scrawl was still printed. As I concentrated on it I realized that one more name had to be added to make it complete and provide the final, ironic message. Walking over to the board I erased the words, then picked up the chalk and began to write.

"What on earth are you doing?" John asked, but I did not answer. I simply stepped back, allowing him to read:

THEDGEHUGHES, ARNAUGHT, WILBY, BLAMEFORT, NOTTING:
    THE MEN THAT *VURCZAK*.

THE ADVENTURE OF THE DAMSEL IN GREY

"A holiday!" I cried, "John, do you really mean it?"

"Absolutely," my husband answered. "I have already made all the arrangements and cleared my appointment calendar for the next week."

"Darling, what brought this on?"

"I simply came to the conclusion that I have not been giving you the attention you deserve, what between my practice and, well, you know..."

I smiled, knowing indeed.

"... And since we never had a honeymoon as such, I thought that this might make up for it."

"Oh, John!" I sighed, running into his arms, not caring that I must have resembled the twittering witless heroine from a third-rate melodrama. "Where are we going? No, wait, don't tell me. France? Spain?"

"My dear, we are on our way to Nether... "

"The Netherlands! How delightful!"

John cleared his throat self-consciously. "Actually, Amelia, we are going to Nether Sworthing."

"We are going *where*, dear?"

"Nether Sworthing. It is a delightful little village in the Cotswolds, a mere two-hour journey by train."

I stepped back from his embrace, trying to mask my disappointment with a frozen smile. "And where did you hear about this Swollen Nothing?"

"*Nether Sworthing*," John corrected, though I had heard him perfectly well the first time. Sarcasm, alas, is frequently lost on my husband. "I was there a number of years ago, with Holmes, working on a case."

"I should have guessed," I said. While there are many

privileges in being the wife of Dr. John H. Watson, albeit the second to hold the title, the ever-present umbra of Mr. Sherlock Holmes, which looms over us like the overpowering memory of a cherished first wife, is not one of them.

It is not that I dislike Mr. Holmes. In my few, undeniably eventful experiences with him, he has struck me as being entirely too vulnerable to truly dislike, despite that carefully formed veneer of cold rationality. On one or two occasions he has even shown me great kindness, which, I understand, is quite singular (to use John's favourite word) in his history of dealings with the opposite sex. But those few instances are weighed against the many evenings I have spent alone and desperately lonely, waiting for my husband to return from his latest Holmesian escapade, vainly wishing that the "world's greatest detective" would retire and let us conduct our own lives in peace.

My sudden change of mood at the mention of Holmes' name should have been palpable to anyone, though John remained oblivious, continuing to prattle on about this particular Cotswold Eden.

"... And the next thing I know, I get a letter from this fellow Reeves, whom Holmes and I met there years ago, stating that he has taken over the village inn and inviting me down to stay with him. And I thought: 'What a superb idea!' The village is peaceful, quiet and charming, the perfect place to leave the problems of the great city behind and just relax. You will love it, Amelia, I promise."

Honestly, how could I continue to be cross with him when he was trying so valiantly to please me? "I will do my best to adore the place, darling," I said, and I meant it.

Three days later we boarded the train at Paddington, and after a refreshingly uneventful journey, stepped off at the station in Moreton-at-Marsh, which was as close as we could get by rail to Nether Sworthing. No sooner had John wrestled our bags to the platform when a voice called: "Ho! Dr. Watson! Over here!"

"Reeves!" John called back, hailing a tall, powerful looking man who was dressed for the country in tweeds and a deerstalker cap (Heaven help us!), the latter evenly perched atop his woolly head. Gabriel Reeves sprinted to us, grabbed John's hand and shook it vigorously. "What a pleasure to see you again, doctor!" he bellowed. Having pumped John's hand dry, he turned to me and grinned broadly. "And you must be Mrs. Watson. Your servant, madam," he said, taking my gloved hand and kissing in an awkward fashion that indicated he was not very experienced in such greetings.

Largely through Mr. Reeves' efforts our bags were hauled across the platform and loaded onto a stately landau, which was being driven by a boy who looked barely old enough to handle the reins, but proved to be quite capable once we were underway. Within minutes we were enjoying the warm inviting green of the countryside.

Whatever the peculiarities of its name, Nether Sworthing was a beautiful little village, abounding in scenery that would have inspired a landscape painter from the Royal Academy. An arching stone bridge spanned a gently flowing stream, which in turn coursed past rows of compact stone cottages. In the centre of the village sat an ancient market cross and resting atop a nearby green rise was an equally ancient church.

Leaning towards us, Mr. Reeves said: "Norman."

"No, *John*," replied my husband, "though I rarely stand on formality. Just plain Watson will do."

"I believe he means the church, darling," I said.

"That's right," Reeves acknowledged, "it was built in 1163 and is as fine an example of Norman architecture as you will find anywhere in England. Ah, here we are."

The carriage stopped in front of a two-story stone building identified as The Commonwealth Inn. As John helped me down, Mr. Reeves and the driver began to take our bags inside.

The public house of the inn was surprisingly dark and musty smelling, a dreary atmosphere that was brightened only by the sunny demeanor of a plump, cheerful woman whom our host introduced as his "ladywife," Emily. We proceeded upstairs to our room which, although small, was certainly comfortable and offered a pleasing view of the village. After the youthful driver had brought up the last of our bags, John withdrew a sixpence from his pocket and handed it to him.

"Thank you, Dr. Watson, sir," the lad responded.

John studied him. "How did you know my name?"

"Oh, I remember you right well, sir, you and Mr. Holmes. Why, he paid me a shilling for each message I carried for him when you and he was here before."

"Good heavens, you must be young Daniel!" John said, delighted at the discovery. "I never would have recognized you. What a strapping young fellow you've become!"

"Thank you, sir," Daniel beamed. "If there's anything else you'll be requiring while you're here, you just let me know." In an awkwardly earnest parody of a military about-face, the young man spun on his heel and strode away.

"Well, it appears that Mr. Holmes has urchins at his disposal in every corner of the realm."

"I can hardly believe it is the same lad! I must write Holmes immediately and tell him."

"You will do no such thing. We are here to enjoy ourselves, *by* ourselves. There will be plenty to tell Mr. Holmes after we've returned to London." If only I had realized then how prophetic that statement would be!

After unpacking and settling in, we returned to the public house, which was now open and already populated by a handful of customers. As soon as he saw John, Mr. Reeves pumped a glass of dark, cloudy bitter and held it out. "Here, Dr. Watson, try this," he said. "I'm trying my hand at brewing my own, and I'd be interested in your opinion."

John took a sip and his expression told all, though he managed to remain polite. "It's... uh... it's very interesting, though perhaps a bit strong."

"It makes a decent shandy, though," Mrs. Reeves said, wiping her plump hands on her apron as she joined her husband behind the bar. "Can I get you one, luv?"

"Oh, no thank you," I replied. Shandy, in my opinion, was loathsome enough when it was made with good beer.

After few more patrons had entered the pub our host shattered the calm by loudly introducing John as *the* Dr. John Watson of London, friend and chronicler of the great and wondrous Mr. Sherlock Holmes! Suddenly John was the centre of attention, though if he felt uncomfortable in that position, he certainly did not show it.

If nothing else, my years as an ingenue on the amateur stage had taught me when to make an exit, and as I did not particularly wish to spend the rest of the day listening to the baldly romanticized adventures of Mr. Sherlock Holmes, I decided to take advantage of my *exeunt* cue.

"Mrs. Reeves," I called, motioning her to me, "would you be so good as to tell me what there is to see in your village."

"See? In Nether Sworthing?" she laughed. "The church is about the only thing worth seeing, luv. It should be open now, though if it isn't, just knock up the sexton and he'll let you in."

"Thank you. And could you please let my husband know that I went out for a bit? He appears to be a tad preoccupied at the moment." With that, I slipped outside.

Finding the church posed no problem, since it was visible from every part of the village. Just as Mrs. Reeves had predicted, the doors were indeed open. As I crept inside, a chill came over me, not a dankness like the one I had left behind in the pub, but a stony, tomblike cold. Still, the little church was serenely beautiful, with ornately carved pews and faded frescoes, apparently Norman in origin, adorning the walls. My footsteps echoed back as I walked towards the chancel, seating myself in the front pew. I spent several minutes in reverent silence, enveloped in a stillness so complete that when the sighing voice suddenly came from somewhere behind me, it echoed through the walls like the howling wind.

I turned around a saw a young woman standing at the rear of the church. Her long, dark hair seemed to stand away from her face, as though it were windblown. She was dressed completely in grey and her clothing seemed of a very old fashion. Even from that distance, I could read the expression of fear on her face.

"Help me," she said.

"What is wrong?" I called back.

"My father wants to kill me!"

"What?"

She looked sharply to the side, as though alerted by a sound that I was unable to hear, and with a sudden gasp, bolted from the spot.

"Wait!" I cried, springing out of the pew and running up the aisle. I would swear under oath that at no time had I taken my gaze away from of the spot where the woman had stood, yet when I got there, there was no sign of another human being. The woman had simply vanished.

"This cannot be," I muttered, surveying the interior of the church one more. The woman was nowhere to be found.

Leaving the church, I practically ran back to the public house, trying to shake off the cold, uneasy feeling that had overtaken me. Upon returning, I found that John was still enjoying his position centre stage and was relating one of his more recently published stories, a wild tale of a mad dog running loose on the moors. My distress must have shown as I made my way to the bar, since our host asked: "Mrs. Watson, are you all right?"

"I've had the most extraordinary experience," I said. "I was sitting in the church, alone, I thought, and this young woman came in, dressed completely in grey, and she asked for my help."

"You've seen her, then?" Mr. Reeves interjected, loudly and urgently enough to silence my husband, who asked: "Is something wrong?"

"I don't know," I said. "There was a young woman in the church who seemed distressed and frightened, and she said that her father wanted to kill her."

A low chorus of murmuring went through the pub, and I quickly realized that all eyes had turned away from John and were now focused on me.

"She obviously needs help," I went on, "we must find her."

"I'm afraid you're too late," Mr. Reeves said, matter-of-factly. "Her father was the squire of Nether Sworthing, and in a drunken rage over her elopement to a commoner, he did kill her... more than a hundred and fifty years ago."

"I'm afraid I don't understand."

"You have seen the Damsel in Grey, Mrs. Watson, our local ghost."

Suddenly exhausted, and more than a little confused, I quickly retired to our room. But by that evening the story of my encounter with the "ghost" had spread over the village like a flooding river, and even our attempt to take our dinner was so interrupted by locals asking for details of my "sighting," that Mr. Reeves finally had to intervene.

The situation was even worse on the following day when our every movement was tracked by a small army of local cottagers, all hoping to be present should the phantom make a return appearance. My repeated attempts to explain that I did not even believe in the existence of ghosts fell on deaf ears, and hopes of enjoying relaxing holiday in the country had vanished as completely as the Damsel herself.

As we prepared for bed at the end of our second day as visiting curiosities, John glumly suggested: "Why don't we tell everyone that it was a mistake, that you really saw nothing at all."

"I fear it has spread too far, no one in the village would believe that now. Besides, it was *not* a mistake. I did see that girl."

"What a singular problem," John sighed. "I wonder what Holmes would make of it?"

"And you will continue to wonder, darling, in complete silence, if you have any hopes of turning this into a honeymoon," I replied, climbing into the large, downy bed.

We slept comfortably. Early the next morning, however, we were awakened by a commotion outside our room, punctuated by someone pounding on our door and crying, "Dr. Watson! Dr. Watson!"

"What on earth... " John muttered, climbing out of bed and skipping over the cold floor while trying to get his arms in his robe. Opening the door, he found Daniel.

"Come quick, sir, there's been an accident!"

"Let me get dressed. I'll be right down." We both dressed in record time, though the improperly aligned buttons of John's shirt advertised his haste. Daniel rushed us outside where a horrible sight was waiting for us. The body of a young woman lay crumpled in a small garden at the side of the inn. Upon seeing her face, I gasped. "It's she!" I shouted. "That is the woman I saw in the church!"

"Great Scott!" John cried. "Are you sure?"

Bracing myself, I knelt down to examine her more closely. A modern shirtwaist and skirt had replaced the archaic grey dress, and most of her left temple was discoloured by dark, ugly bruise, but even so, there was no mistaking her. "I am positive," I said. "This is the Damsel in Grey."

"Well, this woman certainly did not die a hundred-and-fifty years ago," John replied. "She's been dead for maybe six or seven hours."

I had started to rise again when I detected a peculiar odour — peculiar, at least for the circumstances. I leaned down until my nose was just above her blouse.

"Amelia, what on earth are you doing?" John asked.

"Lemon. I detect the scent of lemon on her clothes."

"What can that possibly mean?"

"I'm sure I don't know, but —"

My thoughts were interrupted by the sudden reappearance of Daniel, who notified John that the constable from the neighbouring village had been sent for. "So, sir," he added, "have you figured out how she was killed?"

"Blow to the head, I should think."

"Hmmm, or maybe a fall from a height," Daniel said, directing our attention to an open second-floor window above where the body lay. "She might have fallen from that window and hit her head on one of these rocks."

"Yes, Daniel, I daresay you could be right," John said, clearly impressed by the deduction. "Now, if you could only tell us who she is."

"Her name is Sarah Wells," said another voice said, and I looked up to see the ashen, stunned face of our host, Mr. Reeves. "Come inside, please, and I will tell you everything."

"Daniel, see if you can find a blanket to cover her with until the police arrive," John said, and the lad sprinted away. I remained where I was, having discovered another puzzling element. "I'll be there in a second, dear," I called to John, "I want to catch my breath first."

Within seconds Daniel had returned with the blanket, which smelled like a stable. "Best I could do on quick notice," he confessed.

"Daniel, what do you make of these?" I asked, fingering

two depressions in the ground.

"Looks like footprints, only deeper."

"My thoughts exactly. Would you mind terribly holding up her leg?" He did as I asked, with no outward sign of discomfort, which was more than I could say for myself as I gingerly slipped off one of the dead woman's shoes. It fit perfectly into one of the depressions. "This matter gets more puzzling by the second," I noted.

"How so, ma'am?"

"Because of the depth of the prints. The ground isn't wet or spongy enough for her feet to have sunk down into it. She would have had to hit the ground with great force to make these marks."

"Right, like if she fell out of a window."

"But only if she fell *feet first*. Yet the wound on her temple implies she landed head first. How can a person do both at the same time? Unless..."

"Unless?"

The only possible explanation was not a very pleasant one to contemplate. "I will have to explain later," I said, "now I must now rejoin my husband. And for the time being, Daniel, let's not tell anyone else about these footprints, all right?"

"If you say so, ma'am."

I left him to cover the body of poor Sarah and stepped to the door of the public house, which was quickly opened by Mrs. Reeves. Once I was inside, she equally quickly closed and locked it again. Her husband was slumped down in a chair and still ashen. "I honestly saw no harm in the deception," he said.

"What have I missed?" I asked.

I could tell from John's manner that something in our host's statement thus far had already irritated him. "It seems," he began, "that we have been the victims of an insidious prank. That poor girl now lying dead was an actress from London, hired by Reeves to impersonate the ghost specifically for our benefit."

"Oh, good heavens," I cried. "But why our benefit?"

Never taking his gaze from the floor, Mr. Reeves said, meekly: "I though we might be able to fire up Dr. Watson's imagination enough that he would write a Sherlock Holmes story centered around our local legend, like he did with the hound of Dartmoor."

"My imagination!" John roared. "My dear Reeves, the stories I write concerning the exploits of my friend, Mr. Sherlock Holmes, are based on actual facts and not the products of my imagination!"

"Gently, darling, gently," I said, trying to calm him down.

Then turning to the innkeeper, I asked: "But even if he were to write such a tale, how would that benefit you?"

"By drawing tourists into the village. Interest in spiritualism is growing. Once the reading public learned of an actual, documented ghostly sighting, presented by a reputable author, people would flock to Nether Sworthing, hoping for the chance to see the Damsel for herself. And they would, by necessity, take lodging here at the inn."

"And that was why you invited us up here," John said, bitterly. "You were merely using us as part of this bizarre plan."

"Dr. Watson, every farthing I own has been sunk into this lodging house and the return has not been forthcoming," Reeves declared. "I had to do something. And it would have worked, if only poor Sarah hadn't panicked."

"I don't follow you," John said.

The innkeeper sighed deeply. "Of the actresses I interviewed in the city, Sarah was the most desperate for work. She said she would do anything for a job and agreed to come here without fully realizing what would be required of her. You see, in order for her appearances as the Damsel to be effective, she had to remain hidden at all other times. We lodged her upstairs and forbade her to leave her room, under penalty of forfeiting her pay. Meals and other necessities were brought up to her. At first, she occupied her time studying the legend of the Damsel and perfecting her performance, but then she became restless. Even one day can seem like an eternity when it is spent shut in and alone."

Reeves finally faced us directly, all life seeming to have drained from his eyes. "After a while she became careless," he went on. "She began to slip out in the evenings when she thought we were asleep. I caught her one night near the church. Fortunately, nobody else had seen her, but I could no longer afford to take chances. After that, we started locking her in her room."

"Good lord," John muttered.

"There was no alternative, doctor. We thought it would prevent any further attempts at escape until her role, as it were, had been completed. Her time finally came when your wife said she wanted to see the church. As soon as you gone, Mrs. Watson, Emily went upstairs and told Sarah to get ready, and while you were holding the attention of the customers, doctor, Em slipped Sarah out the back door and took her to the church. After her appearance as the Damsel, she hid in the church and remained there until after dark, when I was able to go get her. By then, though, she'd managed to get herself all worked up. She demanded her money, saying she'd had enough of the village, the Damsel and the whole plan, and wanted to leave as soon as possible. There was nothing I could do but agree. I told her I would pay her off as soon as we were back at the inn. But once I had gotten her here..." his voice began to falter.

"You locked her back inside her room," John said, and the innkeeper nodded, saying: "I wanted one more appearance before I let her go. It didn't even dawn on me that she might try to get out through the window."

"So you think she fell to her death during an escape attempt?"

"That is what I believe, may God have mercy on her soul, and mine, too."

The sound of the door opening prevented me from giving the wretched man a very large piece of my mind regarding his irresponsible and callous behaviour towards a poor unfortunate girl. A stout, smug looking police constable sauntered into the public house, quickly followed by Daniel, who announced, "This is Constable Trout."

"I'll take it from here, son, if you don't mind," the policeman said, puffing up his chest. "Now then, let's just start from the beginning, if you please."

As the story was tumbling out once more I slipped unobtrusively to Daniel's side and in a hushed voice said: "I distinctly noticed that Mrs. Reeves locked the door after I came in. How did you get in just now?"

"Mr. Reeves gave me a master key when I started working for him," he answered.

It took a fair amount of wheedling, but I finally managed to persuade Daniel to let me borrow the key. Constable Trout — who, save for his heavy-lidded eyes, rather resembled one — was now harrumphing mightily and looking in my direction. "If *I* may be permitted to speak now, madam?" he blustered. "This looks to me like an open-and-shut case of accidental death, though I assure you I shall be fully apprising my superiors of the doubtable actions that resulted in this tragedy." He stopped to glare recriminatingly at Mr. and Mrs. Reeves before adding: "And they may have more to say about this."

Rushing to my husband's side, I clapped a hand to my forehead and moaned: "I suddenly feel so faint, help me upstairs, darling."

"We will be in our room should anyone require us further," John announced, then walked me to the stairs. Once we had reached the landing, he whispered: "I hope the stage performances of your youth were more accomplished than that one, my dear.

What are you up to?"

Ignoring his criticism (I felt I had been quite convincing), I proceeded down the hallway, past our own room, and stopped in front of another door, which was locked. "Yes, this must be it."

"Amelia, what the devil are you doing?"

"I want to see the girl's room," I said, producing the master key.

"Where did you get that?" John demanded, but before he could finish his protest I was inside the room. Although the furnishings were identical to those in our room, it was strewn with loose articles of clothing and other clutter, and quite dirty.

"What are you looking for?" John asked, and in truth, I did not know myself, until I found it. "Look at this," I said, crouching down next to a circular spot on the stone hearth, which had recently been washed. It was, in fact, the only clean spot in the entire room.

"Why would someone wash a hearth stone but leave the rest of the place so filthy?" John asked.

I managed to subdue an overpowering urge to say, *Elementary*, answering instead: "To wash off traces of blood, I would imagine."

John's eyes grew wide. "Amelia, do you mean to tell me that —"

"I am convinced Sarah died in this room and was pushed out of the window to make it look like an accident or a suicide. The real question is, who would want to kill her?"

"We had better advise the constable of this before he leaves," John said.

"That pompous baboon? You saw the manner in which he spoke to me. I hardly think he would take my advice about anything. No, darling, I must think this one out for myself. Let's go back to our room."

We left the dead girl's room as surreptitiously as we had entered it, and returned to our own suite. "I must clear my head," I said. "Please hand me that book." As I began perusing *Our Mutual Friend*, by Mr. Dickens, an author whose shining brilliance has always provoked a heightened clarity in my own mind, John decided to lie down.

In between paragraphs I set about thinking over the facts of the tragedy. As I recounted the individual pieces of this bizarre puzzle, many began to fit together. Only one fit nowhere: the puzzling smell of lemon on the dead girl's clothing. "Oh, this is maddening," I muttered, snapping the book shut.

"Are you all right, dear?" came John's voice.

"I'm sorry, darling, I thought you were asleep."

He rolled over on the bed to face me. "How can I sleep when I am tortured by the inescapable conclusion that my friend Reeves is a murderer?"

"Mr. Reeves, John? Do you really think so?"

"Look at the facts, Amelia. A woman is killed inside a room that is always kept locked. That means the killer must have possessed a key. Who other than Reeves would have had a key?"

"Well, Daniel, for one, but why would Daniel... *oh*!" I cried, putting a hand to my head.

"I know that gesture," John said, suddenly sitting up, and it pleased me to detect in him some small trace of the excitement he normally reserved for his exploits with the great Mr. Holmes. "You have figured it all out, haven't you?"

"Yes, darling, I believe I know who killed Sarah, though I pray I am wrong. Come along, I suddenly feel like a drink."

"At this hour?" John protested, but I had already started for the stairs, leaving him no choice but to follow.

Constable Trout had departed, leaving the sombre tableau of our host and hostess and Daniel grimly going about their chores in preparation to open the public house. "I hope we never have to go through that again," the innkeeper said bitterly, as he wiped dry a glass. "That blighter nearly upset my Em to tears."

"He was rather a brute," I concurred. Then turning to Emily Reeves, I said: "I know the bar is not officially open yet, but there has been so much excitement already this morning, I wonder if I could prevail upon you to make a shandy for me. It may help calm my nerves."

"Coming right up, luv," she said, seeming happy to oblige. "I often take a bit o' the stuff myself when I get worked into a frazzle." I watched carefully as she pumped a glass half-full of her husband's noxious bitter. Then from a place underneath the bar she carefully selected three lemons, which she sliced open and squeezed into a separate glass, adding in water and a touch of sugar. She poured this concoction into the beer and set it down in front of me, and wiped her hands on her apron.

"Thank you," I said, forcing myself to take a sip. It was abominable, though I managed to keep a smile on my face (and John dares to question my acting ability!) "This must be just like the one you made right before you dropped Sarah's body out of the window."

"Oh, aye, that was —" Mrs. Reeves stopped suddenly, her face turning pale.

"What are you saying, Mrs. Watson?" her husband demanded.

"Something that gives me no pleasure, I assure you. But you were the one who caused her death, weren't you, Mrs. Reeves?"

"It wasn't my fault, not entirely," she cried. "The poor lamb, being cooped up in that room had driven her half-mad. Getting locked back up after she'd been let out must have been the last straw. She was waiting for me when I took her dinner up that night. She jumped on me, demanding the key. She didn't even want the money, she said, she just wanted to be let out. She tried to choke me." The woman pulled down the high collar of her dress to reveal rows of swollen red scratches.

"Good heavens, those need to be treated," John said, dashing upstairs for the small medical bag he is never without.

"Go on, Mrs. Reeves," I said.

"Well, I fought back, any way that I could. I managed to get my hands under her and I shoved as hard as I could. She went back, all right, back over a table and down, and then I heard this horrible sound... she'd hit her head on the hearth."

John had now returned and was pulling a jar of salve from his bag to dab onto the scratches.

"I knew she was dead," Mrs. Reeves continued, tearfully, "but there were people downstairs. So I locked the door and left her there. Later, after closing, I made myself a shandy for courage and went back up. I thought that maybe I could make it look like an accident after all. I wrapped my apron around her, so's I didn't have to touch her, and drug her over to the window. It took some doing, but I got her through. Then I cleaned up the spot where she'd hit her head and just waited for her to be found in the morning." She dabbed her eyes with the corner of her apron. "How did you know it was me, luv?"

"The smell of lemon was on her clothes," I replied, "something I could not explain until I remembered your offering me a shandy, which is made with lemonade. Your apron that night must have been still damp with lemon juice when you wrapped it around her."

"So am I to go to prison because of a shandy?" she asked, helplessly.

"There is no question that we will have to inform the authorities," John said, "though I think these scratches will present a good case for self-defence. You may count on me to testify on your behalf, when the time comes." Dear, considerate John.

As Gabriel Reeves stoically comforted his sobbing wife, Daniel was dispatched once more to intercept the constable and bring back. There was nothing else for John and I to do but return to our room and begin packing. How differently this holiday had turned out from our original intent!

"I cannot believe all this happened simply because Reeves wanted me to write a ghost story," John said, neatly folding one of his shirts and placing it in the suitcase.

"Never underestimate the power of fiction, darling."

"And that's another thing; it still rankles me that he seems to think I make these stories up! I am simply relating my experiences with Holmes."

"Come now, even you must admit that you have on occasion exaggerated matters."

"Not a bit!"

"Oh, really, John, a disgruntled tenant farmer turns a dog loose on the landowner, and you play it up as the Hound of Hell."

"It *was* a Hound of Hell! At least that's what it looked like in the dark."

I was unable to stifle a giggle, which quickly turned into a spasm of laughter, which further infuriated John, sending him into a prolonged silence. After a time, though, and with a decidedly wicked glint in his eye, he said: "You know, Amelia, perhaps I should write up this little adventure. It was, after all, a singular piece of deduction, and I don't suppose you would really mind if I changed things around to make it Holmes who solved the case, would you?"

"You do that, darling," I purred, giving him a wicked look of my own, "and you might just find yourself relocating back to Baker Street."

THE ADVENTURE OF THE GLASS HOUSE

"Harry!" I cried, "Harry Benbow! Heavens, is it really you?"

The small figure in the cloth cap turned and regarded me for a moment, then his face lit up like a brazier. "Amelia Pettigrew!" he shouted, then practically danced his way through the half-dozen Covent Garden flower carts that separated us. "Little Amelia Pettigrew," he repeated, "*Gor*, I can't believe it!" At first I thought he was going to take me in a mad embrace, which would have all but crushed the bouquet of red roses I was holding, but he settled for clasping my free hand in both of his. "How long has it been?"

"Too long, Harry," I said, "and it is Amelia Watson now."

"No kidding! Our little Amelia found herself a feller, did she? I hope he's not an actor."

"No, Harry, he's a doctor, whose chief fault is polluting the air of our home with his pipe, which is why I am out buying flowers. But tell me, what you are up to."

"Oh, 'bout five-foot-four," he said, as I knew he would, and I laughed, as he knew I would. It was easily twenty years since I had last seen Harry Benbow, at which time we were both in the same amateur theatrical troupe, I being the young (*very* young, mind you) ingenue, while Harry was the lead comedian. But the years had not dimmed his energy, nor his ability to make me laugh.

"I've been doing a bit o' this and that," he went on. "But listen, I'm acting again."

"How wonderful! What theatre?"

"Well, it's not for the theatre, it's for the filums. You know, moving pictures? Surely you've heard about them."

In truth, I knew very little about moving images projected onto a screen. I had heard just enough about them to know that some people considered them a vulgar novelty while others felt they were the future of entertainment. Harry was obviously among the latter.

"This bloke from America, Nick Johnson, his name is, he's doing some picture work over here, so who's the first person he calls? Harry Benbow." His pride was about to burst through his well-worn vest. Then he did a "take" and slapped himself on the forehead with his palm. "*Gor*, it's providence what brought us together today! We need an actress, and here you are! Amelia, how would you like to be in pictures?"

"Me?"

"Sure! We had a girl drop out yesterday and there's a part open now. You'd be perfect for it."

"But Harry, I can't go back to acting, I'm a respectable married woman now."

"Oh, if that's what's bothering you, wait 'til you meet our leading lady. Just come around and meet Mr. Johnson, and if you still say no, then no harm done. The stage is only a quick step up the road from here."

A quick step indeed! My feet were aching by the time we reached a glass hot house, the kind used for growing plants, at the far end of Coram's Field. Even before we had entered the structure, I could hear the sounds of pandemonium inside.

People scurried back and forth in the building, brightly illuminated by the sunlight beaming in through the ridged glass roof. All four walls, though, had been covered with black drapes. At one end of the glass house was a makeshift stage with three wall flats, painted and decorated as a chamber of a grand palace. Standing on this set was a woman dressed, jewelled and bewigged in such a way that could only signify a queen, while hovering around her were three men in soldier uniforms of the Commonwealth era. "Don't tell me, Harry, let me guess: 'The Three Musketeers?'"

"Presented for the first time ever on filum," he said, brightly, "and with a sterling cast, including yours truly as Planchet."

"But why are you doing this in a hot house?"

"The very same question I asked when summoned to become a member of this company, and one that Mr. Johnson put straight. See, the camera needs a lot of light or else nothing shows up on the filum, and the best source of that light is the good ol' sun. Some of the lesser filum companies, I hear tell, builds their sets in the open and then spends the whole day fighting the wind. But our Mr. Johnson, he's a clever one. He sets up inside a glass house, which allows you to let the light in but keeps the breeze out.

Come on, ducks, let me introduce you to him."

Harry led me through the chaos to a man in shirt sleeves who appeared to be the calm in the center of the storm. He was tall — taller even than Mr. Holmes — and was forced to bend nearly in half in order to peer through the eyepiece of a crank-driven contraption that was attached to a three-legged stand, which I presumed to be the moving picture camera. "Mr. Johnson!" Harry called out, literally bouncing up and down like a ball to gain his attention.

"Oh, there you are Harry," the man said in an accent that sounded Irish by way of Canada. Then I remembered Harry telling me the man was an American. "Did you bring the flowers?" he asked.

"Oh, Gor, I forgot!" Harry moaned.

"You may borrow my roses if you need them urgently," I jumped in.

The tall man directed his gaze upon me. "And you are..."

"Mr. Johnson, I have solved our casting problem," Harry announced. "This is Amelia Pettigrew, who would be perfect as Constance."

The producer sized me up toe-to-head. "Have you ever acted before, Miss Pettigrew?" he asked, but before I could answer, Harry chimed in with, "She and I trod the boards together with the Delancey Players," pointedly leaving out the word *amateur*.

"Fine, be here tomorrow morning at nine o'clock sharp," Mr. Johnson said, "and thank you for the flowers." He strode over to a table on the set and placed them in a vase.

"Our Mr. Johnson's a tartar for authenticity," Harry said, admiringly. "No artificial flowers for his filum!"

"But I only offered to *lend* him my roses," I said, plaintively.

"Oh, Amelia, what's a few roses compared to the beginning of a whole new career! Just think of it: Benbow and Pettigrew together again. Look, I've got to go get in costume now, but I'll see you tomorrow." Then like a rubber ball, he bounced into the middle of the chaos and disappeared.

I have to admit that, while my mind was reeling at the pace with which everything had transpired, I found the prospect of performing again rather exciting. How John would have felt about it was another matter, but one in which I could not enquire since he was away, visiting an ailing member of his old army regiment. I journeyed home (on the omnibus this time) to prepare for my debut on the morrow as a "filum" actress!

Arriving at the appointed time the next day, I found the activity in the glass house on even more chaotic. I was immediately taken in hand by Harry, who was wearing an ill-fitting servant's costume, and in short order introduced to four young men in Musketeers uniforms, who appeared more concerned with their dice game than with the production, a gentleman named Maurice Denby, who was enacting the role of the Louis XIII, and an elderly, crouched and rather sour fellow named Faversham, who was essaying the part of Richelieu. Finally we came to the woman I had seen the day before in Queen's raiment.

"This, Amelia, is our star," Harry said, respectfully. "May I present the Lady Ashford, wife of the Right Honorable Earl of Ashford."

"Of the Ashford Diamonds?" I gasped.

"The same," she replied pleasantly, "and I can read on your face the question nearly everyone else has asked: What am I doing in these surroundings?"

I confessed that the question had occurred to me.

"I will tell you, then. A week or so back Mr. Johnson contacted us, inquiring as to whether he could photograph my husband's ancestral home, Notley Court, as a background for his film. Unfortunately, George was rather against it, but then when the young man asked if he could photograph me instead, as the Queen of France, it was simply too flattering to refuse. You see," she said, conspiratorially, "I have long harbored as secret desire to perform."

I had the pleasure of chatting with her for a few more minutes before she and Harry were called away by a sullen, plain-looking young woman who examined and adjusted their costumes. Suddenly left to fend for myself, I did my best to stay out of the way of the people that were dashing back and forth, ultimately deciding that the safest place to stand was next to the moving picture camera itself.

The contraption looked like a tiny steamer trunk with a lens in the front and a crank on the side. Unable to stifle my curiosity, I tested the crank and heard a whirring sound coming from inside the box. Then I heard a voice shouting: "Don't touch that!"

Letting go of the crank, I turned to see Nick Johnson running towards me. "Please, Miss Pettigrew, never touch the camera. If you were to accidentally open the magazine you would expose the film to light and ruin the image, and I'd hate to lose all of the footage we shot yesterday."

"Oh, I am sorry," I stammered.

"You should be getting into costume, anyway. Beryl!" he

called, and the plain young woman reappeared out of the hurly burly. "Beryl, this is our new Constance, please get her dressed."

The girl opened her mouth, as though to protest, but then appeared to think better of it and instead leveled her gaze towards me, giving me a look of extreme disapproval. "Come on, then," she said, turning on her heel and marching towards a row of partitions made of black drapes.

As I trotted behind her I said, "We haven't met. My name is — "

"Costume's in there," she interrupted testily, pulling open one of the drapes. "Get a move on, then." With that, she spun around again and strode away.

Oh, the insolence of youth!

The drapes had done their job well, making the changing area so dark that I could barely read the label marked *Constance* on the ornate dress I was expected to wear. The darkness had also made me unaware that there was another in the dressing area, until a sudden movement alerted my attention.

"Good heavens, you startled me!" I told the figure in what appeared to be a long red dress. Only on closer inspection did I realize that I was sharing the dressing room with a man! He was elderly, crouched and bearded, and clad in a long red robe. The Cardinal Richelieu, no doubt. "I am sorry, I thought I was alone," I said. "My name is — "

"Of little concern to me," he finished in a croaking voice, then limped off towards the opening in the drapes.

"Well, I never!" I called after him, but he was already gone. The major requirement for working in motion pictures, it seemed, was a rude disposition! Since the dressing room (*cell* might be more accurate) appeared to offer all the privacy of Victoria Station, I decided I had best change as quickly as possible. I slipped off my green velveteen dress and donned the costume, which fit, reasonably well, then stepped out into the light to await further instructions.

I was soon called to take my place in a tableau that also included the Queen, King, Cardinal, Musketeers and Harry as the Musketeer's servant. Stepping into our midst, Mr. Johnson explained the scene, which consisted of my removing the Queen's diamond necklace and handing it to her with a curtsey, while she in turn offered it to a kneeling D'Artagnan, as all else reacted. We rehearsed the action, after which Mr. Johnson once more stepped forth.

"When you present the jewels, Lady Ashford, make sure you pause and hold them out in front of you like this," he said, taking the necklace and demonstrating the way he wanted it displayed for the camera. "See how I'm catching the sunlight in the stones? Do it like that." Then handing the necklace back to her, he said, "All right, let's try it," and took his place behind the camera, while Beryl, still in a sulk, watched from the side.

So it went for the entire morning, with one tableau after another set up, explained, rehearsed and then photographed, though how it could be pulled together into a cohesive story was beyond me. Perhaps that was not necessary in moving pictures. After a meagre lunch, which was assembled by the scowling, drudge-like Beryl, the afternoon was spent setting up a sword fight, which for some inexplicable reason was taking place between D'Artagnan and the Cardinal. Had Mr. Johnson even bothered reading Dumas? When the afternoon light became too dim to continue, we were called into a brief meeting to discuss the scenes that would be photographed on the morrow, then dismissed by the producer.

"So, tell me, Amelia," Harry said, as we made our way to our dressing closets, "what did it feel like to hoist a fortune?"

"What do you mean?"

"The Queen's necklace."

My confusion must have shown on my face, since Harry exclaimed: "*Gor*, you mean you didn't know it was the real thing?"

"Harry, are you telling me that those were the Ashford Diamonds?"

"Right enough."

"You were certainly right about Mr. Johnson's taste for realism," I gasped.

"Oh, it's not just that," Harry said, "it's part of Mr. Johnson's publicity strategy. See, the audience in America isn't going to paying to see Maurice Denby or Ralph Faversham, or even Harry Benbow, but they will pay to see the Ashford Diamonds. In a sense, they're the real stars of the picture!"

I was still trying to absorb this revelation as I entered the dressing area, where another, more sinister surprise awaited me. Pinned to my velveteen dress was a hastily scrawled, unsigned note that read: *If you know what is good for you, get out and do not come back!*

I read the note over and over again, foolishly looking for some inner meaning that was not evident in the terse words, but there was none. There was only the threat, and not a veiled one at that! What was I to do? I could not solicit advice from my husband, since he was away. I suddenly realized there was one man in London to whom I could turn, as uncomfortable as I might feel doing so. But discomfort or no, I had made up my mind, and after changing back into my dress I made my way across the green to Wakefield Street, where I hailed a cab to take me to 221b Baker Street.

"He's not returned yet, dear," I was told by Mrs. Hudson, Mr. Holmes's long-suffering landlady, upon inquiring after him, "but seein's how it's you I don't suppose he'd mind if I let you in to wait for him." I agreed to wait, but then almost changed my mind when she opened the door to the cluttered, smoky hovel that the great detective called home. Since papers were strewn over every piece of furniture, I remained standing until I finally heard the urgent footsteps outside the door and was greeted by the sight of Sherlock Holmes roaring into the apartment like a train emerging from a tunnel.

"Mrs. Watson," he said, rushing past me and beginning to rummage through the pile of papers that covered his work desk, "Mrs. Hudson warned me that you were here, though you could not have chosen a worse time to come. I am very busy."

"And I am rather distressed, Mr. Holmes," I said, holding the note out to him. "I received this today."

Seeing that I was not about to leave, he snatched the paper out of my hand with a sigh of impatience. "It seems you have offended someone, imagine that," he commented dryly, with what I read to be a trace of amusement on his face.

I strenuously protested my innocence and gave him a quick history of my recent involvement with the motion picture company, concluding with the appearance of the note. "I am asking you what I should do, Mr. Holmes."

"My advice, Mrs. Watson, is to do exactly what this note exhorts," he replied, handing the slip back. "Do not continue to associate with these people. Actors are a notoriously unstable breed, who knows what might happen."

"But — !"

"Be so good as to close the door behind you on your way out," Sherlock Holmes said, waving me away and turning back to his papers. Close the door I did — with a slam loud enough to be heard in Calcutta.

After finishing a light supper I prepared for bed, my thoughts never very far from the mysterious and threatening note. It had to be the work of that wretched girl Beryl, who had taken an immediate dislike to me for some unfathomable reason, and I vowed to have it out with here the next day. Do not come back indeed!

But when I arrived at the glass house the next morning I saw a small army of uniformed policemen traipsing around the building. The actors, still in their street clothes, were being kept in a herd by two of the constables, while a smallish man in a bowler hat and mackintosh was questioning Mr. Johnson. Naturally, I rushed up to find out what was going on.

A sergeant suddenly stepped in front of me. "Pardon me, ma'am, do you have a connection with this, er, moving picture?"

"Yes I do" I replied, "what on earth has happened?"

"The inspector will take your statement, stand over there, please."

As I took my place with the other actors, I couldn't help noting that the previously pleasant Lady Ashford was not amused. "Harry," I said, sidling up to him, "what is going on?"

"Mr. Johnson arrived this morning and found Beryl Hunter dead, shot through the heart, she was."

"Beryl? Why would anyone shoot Beryl?"

"That's what the coppers want to find out. They say we have to wait here 'til they talk to all of us, even her ladyship."

My attention was suddenly drawn to the covered figure being carried away on a stretcher by two constables. More specifically, to the pattern of the cloth that was hanging down from under the blanket. I broke away from the group and dashed to the stretcher. "Excuse me," I said, "but is that the victim?"

"Aye," murmured the constable at front.

"Could I ask you to pick up the blanket?"

"Here, now!" a voice said from behind, and I turned to see the inspector hurrying towards us. "Who are you?" he asked me, "and what's all this about?"

"My name is Amelia Watson, and I —"

"Any relation to Dr. John Watson?" he interrupted.

"Yes, he is my husband."

"I see," he said, thoughtfully. "I've worked him and Mr. Holmes, on a couple of cases. I'm Inspector Laurie of Scotland Yard, perhaps he's mentioned me."

"No, he hasn't, but how do you do?" I said.

"Hasn't mentioned me, eh?" the inspector muttered, seeming disappointed. "Well, no matter. Now then, why did you stop my men from taking away the body?"

"I would like to examine what the victim is wearing."

The inspector's eyebrows shot up at this request, but he complied without another word, lifting away the blanket himself. I saw what I needed to see, and at the same time felt myself a chill. Beryl was then recovered and carried away.

"What were you looking for?" the inspector asked.

"She is wearing my costume," I said.

"So?"

"So perhaps that bullet was meant for me."

"For you? Do you know of any reason why someone would want to kill you?"

"No, of course not, but yesterday I did receive this." I showed him the threatening note.

"Hmmm. Well, I can't say whether your fears are grounded or not, but if I were you, I'd do just this note advises, go home and don't come back. Just tell the sergeant where we can reach you before you leave."

After providing the desired information, I turned and started to walk back across the green. Soon I was joined by Harry.

"I'm so sorry, ducks," he said, "I feel like I got you all mixed up in this."

"It is hardly your fault, Harry."

He shook his head. "It's a mess, though, ain't it? *Gor*, poor Beryl. She wanted to be up in front of the camera with the rest of us so bad she could taste it, but she just didn't have the stuff."

I stopped walking. "Harry, what are you saying? Beryl wanted to act?"

"More than anything else, I think. And to his credit, Mr. Johnson gave her a tryout, but the results... well, you know, there's good actors, you 'n me, for instance, then there's passable actors, like old Faversham, and then there's duckies and blokes who have no talent."

"And that was Beryl?"

"Well, even that's being generous," Harry said. "As far as talent goes, that poor girl was in debt. She couldn't act, so Mr. Johnson made her the company runner. She did whatever needed to be done."

Suddenly the motivation behind the threatening note became clear. "That would explain Beryl's animosity towards me," I said. "When your first actress dropped out, Beryl must have thought Mr. Johnson would give the role of Constance to her, but then I showed up out of nowhere and snatched the part away from her. The note was her way of getting rid of me, so she could once more claim the part for herself. Obviously, she thought the note had worked, which is why she was wearing my costume." That was all well and good, but it still did not resolve the disturbing question of whether the bullet had been meant for me.

"Amelia, you've shipped out and left me at the dock," Harry said, his face the very picture of comic puzzlement. "What are you talking about?"

"Oh, nothing Harry," I said, smiling at his expression.

Even when he was not trying to, Harry could make me laugh. Changing the subject, I asked, "What do you suppose is going to happen now? Will the production continue?"

"I wish I knew," he sighed. "Nick Johnson is a keen one for angles, but I don't think he counted on this kind of publicity."

To take our minds off the present, we reminisced about better days until we had arrived at the omnibus stop. There I bid Harry a fond goodbye and started the journey home.

Since I had anticipated being gone for the entire day I had given Missy, our maid, the day off, so it was to a quiet, empty suite of rooms that I returned. Not feeling particularly hungry, I took down my favourite volume from the shelf and settled into the armchair, relishing the chance to forget my own problems amidst the travails of Amy Dorrit and her impoverished father. But awash in the brilliance of Mr. Dickens, my own mind began to work more clearly.

Granted, my thoughts were not so much formulating answers as raising questions, and big ones. The biggest of all, of course, was who had killed Beryl, and even more importantly, *why*? The notion that I had been the intended victim faded away as I remembered Harry's comment that Beryl had been shot through the heart, which strongly suggested that the murderer was facing her. Even clad in my costume, I could not imagine anyone mistaking Beryl's size, colouration and features for mine, a fact that only reinforced the poor girl's delusion that she would ultimately be cast in the part of Constance for the remaining photography, for any audience would surely realize the role was being played by two different women.

At that moment something flashed through my mind like a streak of lightning, something that did not make sense, yet at the same time it made a great deal of sense. At once a few of the loose threads began to tie themselves together, but only a few. I felt certain that they key to Beryl's murder was still inside the glass house and I was pretty sure I knew exactly where it was hidden. I paced the sitting room for the best part of an hour to give the police enough time to vacate the crime scene, then set out once more for the glass house.

The structure looked deserted when I arrived, but I walked completely around it, just to make sure. But as I reached out to turn the knob on the door, a hand touched my shoulder. I gasped and spun around, only to see Harry Benbow standing behind me.

"Harry, you frightened the next five years out of me!" I cried. "Why are you still here?"

"Got no place else to go," he said. "I've just been walking around, thinking about Beryl."

"As have I, and I believe I might be able to shed some light on this puzzle. But first I would like to get back inside the stage. Do you suppose it is locked?"

"Only one way to find out."

Fortunately, the door of the glass house had no lock. Squeaking it open, I called "hello" repeatedly, but received only silence in reply. Satisfied that the glass house was empty, I stepped inside, beckoning Harry to follow, and headed straight for the moving picture camera.

"Do you know how to open this thing?" I asked him.

"Oh, you can't, it'll ruin the filum."

"Only if there is any film inside." I examined the camera from every side but could not identify any kind of release lever or button.

"What are you doing, Amelia?"

"Harry, at this moment I am praying that I am right. One, two, *three!*" On three, I pushed the camera as hard as I could, knocking it off balance and sending it crashing to the floor. Upon impact the box broke open, but instead of spilling out ribbons of film, a single glistening object fell to the floor. I reached down and carefully picked up the silver necklace containing the Ashford Diamonds.

"*Gor*, I don't believe it!" Harry said, eyeing the jewels.

But then a third voice echoed through the structure: "I wish you hadn't done that."

Stepping inside the glass house, armed with a revolver, was Nick Johnson. "Throw me the diamonds," he demanded, and there was nothing I could do but comply.

"Mr. Johnson, what is this all about?" Harry panted, raising his hands.

"As you have obviously realized, Miss Pettigrew, an empty camera is the perfect place to hide stolen jewels. Who is going to look inside, for fear of ruining the film? But I'm curious; before I kill you, tell me how you figured this out."

In a shaky voice said: "Yesterday you told me that if the camera were to be opened you would lose all the film you shot the day before. Then you proceeded to photograph an entire second day's worth of tableaus, without running out of film. Although I know very little about photography, common sense told me that this camera either contained an incredible amount of film, or none at all. And the only possible reason for the camera containing none at all was that is was being used as a hiding place for something else."

Michael Mallory

"But I saw Lady Ashford wearing the diamonds this morning," Harry protested.

"I imagine what we saw was a glass replica, isn't that right, Mr. Johnson?" The American nodded. "In fact, you switched the real diamonds for the fakes right in front of us, didn't you, when you were demonstrating to Lady Ashford how to hold the necklace up to the light?"

"You amaze me, Miss Pettigrew."

"My name is Mrs. Watson," I said, with all the defiance I could muster, "and I also imagine that Beryl somehow found out about the switch, so you shot her and then told the police that you had found the body."

"I had to silence her. She was waiting for me this morning, in costume, no less, threatening to blackmail me into giving her a role in the picture. The silly little fool never realized that there *was* no picture, it was simply a means of getting close to the Ashford Diamonds. But because of that idiot girl and the police, I have already missed my ship, and I cannot afford any more delays." He levelled the gun at my heart. "You first, Mrs. Watson, then Harry. Goodbye."

I held my breath, which I feared would be my last, and closed my eyes, seeing only John's face in the darkness. But suddenly the building was filled with a shattering sound as thousands of shards of glass rained down from the ceiling, and a figure in grey dropped down as though from out of the sky, landing directly on the startled Johnson! In the resulting fracas a shot was fired, but it went wild, breaking more glass. Harry then bravely entered the fray, pouncing on Johnson's arm and managing to wrench the gun from his hand, while the grey man delivered a solid punch to the "producer's" jaw, rendering him unconscious. Only when the grey man looked up did I see, much to my surprise, the ancient face of Faversham, the dour actor playing Richelieu. But that was nothing compared to my surprise when the man stood to his full height, peeled away the face and hair of the old actor and revealed himself to be *Sherlock Holmes!*

"Once you have recovered from your general shock, Mrs. Watson," he said, wiping away the remainder of his makeup, "be so good as to fetch the police."

Within the quarter-hour the team of constables, once more under the direction of Inspector Laurie, had returned and were leading the shackled form of Nick Johnson towards a police wagon. After interviewing Mr. Holmes, Harry and myself for nearly another quarter-hour, the inspector pronounced himself satisfied. I, however, was not.

"Mr. Holmes, why did you not reveal yourself to me in the first place?" I demanded.

"I could not take the chance," he answered, casually dabbing his handkerchief to a cut on his hand, the result of crashing through the glass roof. "I had spent a month trailing Johnson and was getting too close to him to risk discovery. It was imperative that my disguise remain impenetrable and since you had managed to see through one of my masquerades in the past, you were the most serious threat to that imperative, which is why I was forced to leave you that melodramatic warning."

"*You* were the one who left the note?" I cried.

"Not that it did any good," he said, "even when you came to me that evening and gave me the chance to reinforce the message in person. I thank the heavens, madam, that most criminals are not so difficult to dissuade as yourself." Then giving one of his electric smiles, Sherlock Holmes bid us both good day and disappeared across the green of Coram's Field.

"*Gor*, I didn't know you were married to *that* Dr. Watson!" Harry said.

"There is a lot you don't know about me, Harry," I replied, "but if you will permit me, I will try to fit in as much as possible tonight at dinner at Simpson's. It is my husband's favourite eating house." Since we both knew that I would be paying, Harry was gallantly reluctant at first, but I managed to persuade him. As it turned out, the dinner at Simpson's was made even more delicious by Harry's company, and we promised to stay in touch.

Two restful days later, John returned home with encouraging news regarding the health of his fellow Northumberland Fusilier. "How I missed you, Amelia," he said, affectionately. "I hope things were not too dull while I was away."

"Oh, you know how it is, darling," I replied, "once more, I managed to survive."

THE ADVENTURE OF
THE ILLUSTRIOUS PATIENT

A loud, jarring ring shattered the quiet of my home, and it was several seconds before I was able to identify the horrid noise as the new telephone that my husband insisted we needed, one whose sound was far louder and more grating than any I had yet encountered. Uncradling the listening mechanism, I held it to my ear and said, "Yes, hello, what is it?" into the mouthpiece.

"Mrs. Watson," said a voice I recognized only too well.

"Mr. Holmes, I do not wish to speak to you," I said firmly.

"I beg your pardon?"

"You should be begging my forgiveness as well."

"Mrs. Watson, I believe you are mistaking —"

"I am mistaking nothing, least of all that hole I found in John's hat after he returned from your latest escapade. A bullet hole, Mr. Holmes, and had it struck one inch lower I would be wearing mourning colours and more than likely find you opposing me in court for the widow's jointure!"

"Mrs. Watson, please —"

"No, Mr. Holmes, I have remained silent far too long. I have managed to put up with your domination of my husband for his sake, but I will not endure it one day longer! You had John during his youth, but I have him now, and I am not going to sit back and watch him slaughtered in the late summer of his life as a result of your foolish police games. I will forbid him to ever see you again if that is what it takes to reclaim my husband. Therefore, Mr. Holmes, I bid you goodbye."

"Please do not disconnect," the voice entreated. "A pretty tirade, madam, I only hope to be present should you decide to reprise it for Sherlock's benefit."

"But... is this not Sherlock Holmes?"

"No, I am Mycroft Holmes, Sherlock's elder brother."

Dear God in Heaven, there were two of them? "I must apologize, Mr. Holmes," I stammered in embarrassment, "but you sound very much like your brother."

"So I have been told. Now then, is the good doctor about?"

"No, he is still at his surgery. Would you like the address?"

"I have the address, thank you, but the matter in which I require his consultation is rather delicate, requiring far greater privacy than a public surgery could offer. When do you expect him home?"

"He usually returns by six o'clock."

"Expect us at six o'clock, then," said Mycroft Holmes. "Oh, and please be so good as to send your young maid Missy away before we get there." The telephone connection broke off. Us, he had said. Obviously I was to be treated to both Mycroft and Sherlock Holmes (*Mycroft* and *Sherlock* — what could their parents have been thinking?), bringing to our doorstep some business so dire that our maid could not be party to it.

I thought of ringing John at his surgery to warn him of our impending Holmes invasion, but decided against it. Instead I informed Missy of her unexpected evening out, news that she accepted a trifle more cheerfully that decorum warranted, I thought. But only after she had gone did a faintly disturbing thought enter my head: I had never before spoken to Mycroft Holmes, never before knew of his existence, in fact. So how was it that he knew we employed a young maid named Missy?

I was still puzzling over this when the knock came at our door, precisely at the stroke of six. Since John had not yet arrived home, I prepared as best I could to handle our visitors alone. Upon opening the door I saw a portly bearded gentleman of roughly sixty, clad in a dark suit and greatcoat and wearing a black slouch hat. While I could detect no resemblance to Sherlock Holmes in the broad, pleasant face, there was something faintly familiar about the man, who regarded me with sparkling blue eyes. "Mr. Holmes, how nice to meet you," I said, offering my hand. At first he seemed uncertain what to do with it, but then smiled and took it in his.

"Do come in," I said, "and let me apologize once more for my earlier outburst."

"Outburst?" he responded, in a voice clearly different from the one I had heard on the telephone. Just then another man appeared behind him, one whose enormous frame nearly blocked out all of the light from the hall. "How do you do, Mrs. Watson," the second man said, "I am Mycroft Holmes." The elder Holmes was easily as tall as his brother, if not taller, though as corpulent as the detective was emaciated. The poor man was panting and sweating profusely, no doubt the result of having forced his bulk up the stairs.

Leading them into the sitting room (our home, unfortunately, does not have a proper drawing room), I bid them be seated. "I prefer standing," replied the man with the beard, giving each "r" sound a Teutonic roll.

"I must, therefore, stand also," Mycroft Holmes said, rather unhappily. Refusing refreshments, both men remained silent until the sound of the front door opening captured their attention. "Ah, that must be the redoubtable Dr. Watson," Mycroft said, pulling an old repeater watch from his pocket, and adding: "Four minutes late."

Excusing myself, I stepped out to the door and greeted John with light kiss on the cheek. "We have visitors, dear," I said.

"Oh?" he said, removing his coat and hat and hanging them on the coat rack. "Who?"

"One is Mycroft Holmes, and the other —"

"Mycroft Holmes! Great Scot, what is he doing here?"

Mr. Holmes then lumbered into view. "I am sure it must be something of a shock, Doctor, to find me out of my natural habitat, the Diogenes Club, but I come on a matter of great importance. There is someone I want you to meet."

We hastened into the sitting room, but as soon as John clapped eyes on the bearded man he froze in place, his jaw dropping. "Your Majesty," he muttered.

"His what?" I cried.

"May I introduce His Royal Majesty King Edward the Seventh," Mycroft Holmes said, and the bearded man nodded curtly.

"Your M-majesty," I stammered, curtseying, rather awkwardly, "please forgive me for not recognizing you."

The King smiled. "That is a tribute to our Mr. Holmes here," he said. "It was he who has taught me how to dress and act unlike a King for those times when I wish to leave the palace."

"With Your Majesty's permission," I said, "I should like to sit down before I faint."

He nodded again and I sank onto the sofa. John however remained standing. "This is, indeed, quite a singular honour," he said. "How may we be of service to Your Majesty?"

"His Majesty is in dire need of medical attention," Mycroft answered.

"Surely there is the Royal Physician."

"For a variety of reasons, we cannot take Sir Francis into

our confidence regarding this matter."

Pulling a cigar from his inner breast pocket, the King bit off the tip and lit it from a match suddenly proffered by Mycroft Holmes. "Doctor Watson," he began, "were you aware of the fact that I nearly died of illness in my thirtieth year?"

"No, sir, I was not," John replied.

"Too true. Then two years ago, shortly before my coronation, I was stricken with appendicitis, which necessitated emergency surgery."

"Thank heavens Your Majesty received prompt attention."

"Indeed," said Mycroft Holmes, "but the point we are striving to make, doctor, is that His Majesty had never enjoyed more public and Parliamentary support as doing those two periods of illness. His Majesty's appendix, in fact, deserves a great deal of credit for pulling this nation from the threat of European isolation, which lingering resentment over the Boer War had cast over us."

"Great Scot," John muttered.

His Majesty blew out a billow of royal smoke. "It is a good idea for kings to be ill from time to time," he said. "That is why I want you to make me sick."

John glanced over at Mycroft, as though asking for a translation. "Make you sick, Your Majesty?"

"As you probably know," Mycroft rejoined, "His Majesty has recently returned from Paris, which was the final step in forging a pact with France and, we hope, Russia."

"Nicky is a good boy, he will agree," the King stated, and upon reflection I realized he was speaking of Tsar Nicholas, one of his many regal descendants.

Obviously uncomfortable from the prolonged period of standing, Mycroft Holmes eased his bulk against the edge of John's writing bureau (which creaked dangerously) and continued: "The goal of this pact is nothing short of ensuring peace in Europe through alliances that will reduce the power and influence of some of our more bellicose neighbours."

"Like Germany," I blurted out, then immediately regretted it, remembering that another of the King's nephews ruled that empire.

But Mycroft Holmes only smiled. "I see you follow world affairs, Mrs. Watson, how admirable." I smiled back, thankful that he had not automatically added *for a woman*, as his brother would no doubt have said. He went on: "Finalizing such a wide-reaching intercontinental accord is a highly delicate matter and one that requires unquestioning support, the kind that His Majesty feels he could rely upon only if he were suddenly taken seriously ill. At present, however, His Majesty has the misfortune of being, to use the vernacular, healthy as a stallion. Therefore, Dr. Watson, we require a drug of some sort that will give His Majesty every symptom of serious illness, be convincing enough to fool the Royal Physician, yet leave no lasting effects. And time is, I am afraid, of the essence. His Majesty is scheduled to make an appearance at a state dinner at the palace on Friday, to which you are both invited, though he will be forced to cancel the appearance because of the illness that you, doctor, will provide him with."

Dinner at Buckingham Palace! My heart leapt at the news! But Friday was the day after tomorrow. "I have nothing to wear, to the Palace," I blurted out.

Mycroft Holmes smiled once more. "I shall have one of the court dressmakers contact you," he said. "A carriage will come to pick you up Friday at eight o'clock sharp, so please be ready. The fate of Europe is in your hands Doctor Watson. Do not let us down." Then turning to the King, he added, "I believe our task is finished here, Your Majesty." As we bowed to the Sovereign, Mr. Holmes lumbered to the door, opened it and looked out to see if anyone else was present. Satisfied, then motioned for the King to follow him.

My head was absolutely spinning from this unexpected visit. "I did not realize, darling, that you had friends in such high places."

"Frankly, neither did I," John replied. "Oh, I knew that Mycroft worked for the government, and Holmes once remarked that at times when he thought his brother *was* the government, but I never took the comment seriously. Well, my dear, if I am commanded to make the King ill, I had better get to it."

John spent the rest of the evening pouring over medical books and dictionaries, stopping only for strong coffee or to refill his pipe. He was still at it when I finally went to bed some time after midnight, taking a book with me (and while Mr. Dickens remains one of the loves of my life, he is an altogether poor substitute for my husband in bed). I read until my eyes could no longer focus on the words, at which point I set aside my book and extinguished the light, hoping John would soon join me. The next thing I knew, however, the morning light was creeping through the bedroom curtains. I reached for John, finding only cold, empty sheets.

Pulling my warm robe around me, I made my way to the sitting room where I found a note in John's hand on the table, informing me that he had already dressed and gone out, hoping an early morning walk would clear his mind.

Mid-way through my lonely breakfast the wretched telephone jangled again, startling Missy so badly that the poor girl nearly dropped her tray. Once again it was Mycroft Holmes on the line, this time ringing to tell me when to expect the dress fitters. My excitement steadily rose until some hours later, when a prim woman and her young assistant arrived, laden with materials of all kinds and colours. I selected a stylish dark green velvet and was assured that, incredibly, the gown would be ready on the morrow.

The rest of the day passed uneventfully until John arrived home from his surgery, so thoroughly exhausted that he was barely able to stay awake through dinner. "Really, darling, you must get some sleep," I said as I poured him an after-dinner whisky.

"I intend to," he yawned, "because I believe I have finally found the answer. I pray so, anyway."

True to his word, the poor dear slept that night like a hibernating bear, though I tossed and turned, far too excited to sleep. What was the Palace like? I wondered. And what other dignitaries and nobles would be at the dinner? At some point, though, I dropped off into a deep, dreamless slumber from which I was awakened very late the next morning by Missy, after John had already left for the day. My beautiful new evening gown was delivered shortly before tea, and by the time John returned home I was already coiffed and bejewelled for the evening's festivities.

At precisely the appointed time a coach appeared at the curb and we enjoyed a peaceful ride through the city to Buckingham Palace. Although looking elegantly handsome as always in his evening clothes, John seemed lost in a dark, troubled cloud of thought. I felt my excitement returning fourfold as we entered the palace gardens and passed through stately iron gates which opened upon the eastern forecourt, where a queue of like vehicles slowly progressed up the carriage drive. Our coach, however, did not follow the others but suddenly veered around them and took us to a private door at the grounds side of the palace, where the unmistakable form of Mycroft Holmes was waiting.

"Come this way, please," he said as we stepped down from the coach, John helping me down with one hand while clutching his medical bag with the other. I heard the sounds of a spirited gathering coming from somewhere inside the palace as John and I followed Mycroft up a back staircase and down a hallway, finally coming to a closed door. Giving a quick, rhythmic rap, Mycroft awaited the reply then led us in. To our utter shock, we found ourselves in the King's private bedroom!

Save for the crossed swords and crest that were affixed rather melodramatically to one wall, the room was tastefully and simply decorated in a white and gold motif. In the centre of the room the King, now in official raiment, was holding court over a small group of people. Standing just behind His Majesty was a handsome young officer whom Mycroft introduced to us as Lieutenant Benjamin Breakstone, the King's equerry. Next we were introduced to Lord Landsdowne, the Foreign Secretary, and a man who carried himself with great portentousness, as though he was posing for an official portrait at all times. The only other woman, aside from myself, was a coquettish young thing whose dimpled smile was perpetually fixed upon His Majesty, who frequently returned the attention. "May I present Mademoiselle Perrault, whom His Majesty met on his recent trip to Paris," Mycroft said. He needed to say no more, since I recalled the tales I had heard during my days in the theatre regarding the then-Prince of Wales' devotion to beautiful women, most notably the actress, Mrs. Langtry. Obviously, his coronation had done as little to rein in this behaviour in His Majesty as had his marriage.

There was another figure in the room, a tall, thin man whose back was turned to us in order to examine a large oil portrait hanging on the far wall. When the man faced us, my heart sank. "Of course you know my brother, Sherlock," said Mycroft Holmes, as the detective bowed to us.

"I did not realize Mr. Holmes was party to this little deception," I said, striving to maintain civility.

"Oh yes, it was Sherlock who suggested that we turn to your husband, he not having the proper medical knowledge himself," Mycroft answered.

I was about to challenge that statement, knowing of Mr. Holmes obsession with poisons, as well as just about any other manner of death and destruction, when Mademoiselle Perrault suddenly lunged for the King, brazenly touching his arm and shoulder with satin-gloved hands. "Must you go through with this Your Majesty?" she cooed, "it sounds so dangerous." In her accent, the last word came out *don-joor-aus*.

"I have been told I may trust Doctor Watson completely," the King replied. "Shall we be about it, then?"

"Very well, Your Majesty," John replied crisply, and for the first time I saw in my husband a vestige of the former soldier, a man trained to carry out his orders. He opened his bag and took out a small vial of liquid. "This is a solution distilled from tincture of ipecac, which is normally used to induce regurgitation for someone who has swallowed poison."

"Will this solution in any way harm His Majesty?" Lieutenant Breakstone snapped.

"If too much were to be given, yes," John replied, withdrawing a needle from his bag, "but in the correct dosage, it will simply make His Majesty sick, as he requested."

"For your sake, sir, you had better be right," the equerry

said fiercely.

Ignoring the implied threat from Lieutenant Breakstone, John went about drawing up a small amount of the solution into the needle, then offered the vial to Mycroft. "Please take this and do what you will with it," he said, then placed the needle on a small silver tray, set it down on an antique French table, then faced the King. "By preparing this solution, Your Majesty, I have done as you commanded. However, at no time was I instructed to actually administer the dose. Therefore, in lieu of the oath I took as a medical man and the regard in which I hold the Crown, I respectfully refuse to do so unless so ordered by your gracious self."

The King's eyebrows shot up at this and he looked to Mycroft Holmes, whose face bore an inscrutable expression. I prayed that in following his conscience, John had not overstepped his bounds!

The terrible silence that followed was shattered by Sherlock Holmes. "With Your Majesty's permission, I will administer the dose in place of my friend."

"You, Mr. Holmes?" the equerry said, skeptically.

"Oh, don't worry, he has ample experience with needles," I said, only to receive an elbow nudge from my husband.

Carefully picking the tray, Sherlock Holmes examined the needle, then bid His Majesty to roll up his sleeve. But even as this was taking place, a loud *bang*! was heard just outside the door to the King's chambers. "Good Lord, that sounded like a gunshot!" Lord Landsdowne exclaimed.

"Everyone stay here," Sherlock Holmes ordered, setting down the needle and dashing to the door. The confusion that followed lasted only a brief minute before Holmes returned, carefully holding out the remnants of an exploded firecracker.

The King sighed. "My grandson David's work, no doubt. He rather enjoys creating a commotion. Carry on, Mr. Holmes."

As the rest of us looked on (save for Mademoiselle Perrault, who turned away), Mr. Holmes injected the solution into the arm of the King, who did not so much as wince, then placed the needle back on the tray.

"How quickly will the symptoms emerge, doctor?" Mycroft asked.

"Nausea will occur very quickly," John responded, "followed by fatigue and lightheadedness."

"My brother and I will stay with His Majesty until the first signs of sickness occur, then send for the Royal Physician, for show, you understand. The rest of you go downstairs and enjoy the dinner. Lord Landsdowne, would you be so good as to lead our guests to the ballroom?"

It was Lieutenant Breakstone, however, who took command, marching us through a series of magnificent hallways, while Lord Landsdowne engaged Mme. Perrault in conversation, frequently in French. Before long we arrived at the ornately crafted Grand Staircase and continued on a path that eventually led us to the chandelier-filled ballroom. We took our seats at the lavishly set banquet table and chatted amiably with our fellow diners through the first course, which consisted of an excellent turtle soup. Halfway through the pheasant, however, I noticed John's gaze suddenly focus on a man rushing towards the table. "Good heavens, that is Lacking," he said.

"I am hard-pressed to find anything lacking, darling," I responded.

"No, Sir Francis Lacking, the Royal Physician, and judging from his expression, something has gone wrong."

I felt myself go cold as he spoke those words, and watched as Sir Francis rushed to the chair occupied by Lord Landsdowne and demanded that he come with him. This likewise attracted the attention of the King's equerry and Mademoiselle Perrault (whose very presence at the table I felt to be a brazen slap in the face of the Queen). Those two quickly rose and went with Holmes and Sir Francis, and after a quick flurry of pardons to those sitting nearest us, John and I followed.

We arrived en masse to the King's bedroom, each of us, I think, shocked at what we saw. The King was lying motionless in the large canopy bed, his robust countenance now pale and waxen, his eyes open but vacant, and his breathing so shallow as to go unnoticed.

"Dear heavens," I exclaimed, "is he —"

"His Majesty is still alive," said Sir Francis, "though for how much longer I cannot say. Mr. Holmes has already informed me of this foolish scheme." He then turned to John. "You sir, what in God's name could you have been thinking to agree to such an abominable plan? And what did you inject into His Majesty?"

"It was ipecac," John answered, "and I assure you, sir, that the dosage I prescribed would not harm His Majesty. Surely you must realize, Sir Francis, that even an overdose of ipecac would cause convulsions, not lethargy. May I please examine His Majesty myself?"

"No, sir, you have done quite enough," Sir Francis replied icily.

Suddenly frightened for my husband, I turned to Mycroft Holmes. "Please, Mr. Holmes, do something, say something."

"It is out of my hands now, Mrs. Watson," he replied, casually. "I am sorry."

"Out of your hands?" I shouted. "May I remind you, sir, that you were the instigator of this little charade!"

"Mrs. Watson, pray control yourself," broke in the calm, steady voice of Sherlock Holmes. "I ask everyone to refrain from jumping to conclusions. Remember, it was I who administered the dose, not Dr. Watson. Furthermore, he is quite right in stating that the toxin he distilled for injection would not cause the symptoms you see before you, which leads us to only one conclusion: that the King has been injected with another kind of toxin."

"That's impossible, Holmes!" John cried. "I filled the needle myself!"

"True. But if you recall, just as I was preparing to inject His Majesty, a firecracker exploded in the hall. I returned the needle to its tray and went out to investigate. In the confusion that followed, it would have been easy for anyone in this room to tamper with the needle, replacing the innocuous solution with a deadly one."

"Sir, are you accusing one of us?" bristled Lord Landsdowne.

"I am, my Lord, and furthermore, I have taken steps that will clearly reveal the guilty party." After this pronouncement the room fell silent as a tomb. Holmes went on: "Immediately after I relieved Watson of the needle, I took the liberty of coating it with a special chemical that reacts with the natural oils found on the human skin." He then raised his hand for all to see. There were traces of bright orange on his fingers. "Anyone else who touched it will likewise be marked. I would like to examine the hands of everyone in this room."

Mycroft was the first to present his hands, followed by John, then myself (though I could hardly be considered a suspect). Lieutenant Breakstone presented his hands in a strange kind of snapping salute, first showing his palms, then the backs, and then the palms again. After a fair amount of grumbling, Lord Landsdowne offered his hands for view, as did a petulant Mademoiselle Perrault. The last to follow suit was Sir Francis Lacking, who appeared highly insulted at the very request. No one's hands bore any trace of chemical staining.

"Rather blows your theory out of the water, Holmes," Lord Landsdowne said, somewhat nervously. But then I remembered something.

"Mr. Holmes, how would this chemical of yours affect satin?"

"It would not discolour the cloth but would produce a visible stain."

"I suggest, then, that we locate the gloves I noticed Mademoiselle Perrault wearing earlier this evening and inspect them for stains."

"How dare you?" the woman cried, racing for the door. But Lord Landsdowne got there first and braced himself against it to prevent her from leaving. Meanwhile, Lieutenant Breakstone quickly searched the room. As he peered behind a drape near where Mme. Perrault had earlier been standing, he shouted: "Here they are!"

"The game is up, mademoiselle," said Mycroft, a strangely satisfied smile on his face. "Or should I say Fraulein."

The kittenish facade vanished immediately from the young woman and her face became hard and cold. "You may say whatever you like," she answered in a low, emotionless voice which now bore no trace of a French accent, "it will do nothing to bring back your King. The nicotine sulfate will act quickly. So, congratulations, Mr. Holmes, you have me. But you have lost the game. Your swinish sovereign is dead."

Just then another voice filled the room. "Swinish? Really, Marie, you have cut me to the quick," it said, and I gasped to see His Majesty King Edward VII enter the room from a side door! "They tried to warn me that you were a spy," the King said with sadness, "but I refused to believe it."

As I stared at the silent figure in the bed, Mycroft Holmes (who seemed capable of reading thoughts) leaned over and said, "On loan from Madame Tussaud's."

"Would someone please tell me what is going on here?" John cried, but before anyone could answer, the faux Mme. Perrault dashed to the pair of swords that adorned the wall and wrenched one loose. The blade whistled as she sliced it through the air and levelled its razor sharp point directly against His Majesty's throat! "You shall not trick your way out of death this time!" she cried.

"Lieutenant, draw your weapon!" I demanded, but like everyone else in the room, he stood frozen, his face showing all too well the turmoil going on inside of him. "Madam," he practically whimpered, "how, as an Englishman, can I take arms against a woman?"

"Indeed," Mme. Perrault sneered, "what fine English gentleman would lift a finger to harm a lady?"

"None," I shouted, lunging for the crest and pulling down the matching sword. "For that you need a fine English woman! *En garde*, mademoiselle!"

I charged Mme. Perrault, which at least forced her to remove the point from His Majesty's throat long enough to parry my thrust. Heavens, how many years had it been since I last held a sword? Not since old Laurence Delancey, the manager of my former theatrical troupe, had insisted that everyone in his company, even the women, learn the art of stage fencing. But fencing in the theatre and fighting for your life with a sword were worlds apart, as I was now learning.

Mme. Perrault thrust her blade at me so relentlessly that all I could do was repeatedly sidestep its point, and what few effective parries I was able to make were more the result of accident than design. With each new thrust I expected to feel the sharp steel enter my skin, but up to now the real victim was my beautiful gown, which suffered rip after rip at the hands of my opponent. Underneath the loud clanking of blades I could hear John's panicked voice calling, "For God's sake, Amelia, be careful!" Then in my memory I heard another voice, that of Mr. Delancey proudly explaining a move of his own devising, designed to disarm the opponent — on stage, anyway. Still, what other options had I?

I continued to slash away, managing to parry thrust after thrust, waiting for my moment, which finally came when Mme. Perrault overextended herself on a lunge and momentarily lost her balance. As hard as I could, I beat at her blade from the right side, knowing she would counter-parry, then dipped under her sword and beat it again from the opposite direction, a move that served to weaken an opponent's grip. Then with a forward lunge I engaged her blade in an *envelopè*, encircling it once, twice, and on the third twirl, twisted my wrist around sharply, which wrenched the sword from her hand, sending it flying through the air. Her utter shock at being disarmed gave me ample opportunity to level the point of my blade at her midriff. Within a second, Sherlock Holmes had produced a set of handcuffs and in quick order Mme. Perrault was securely bound, though furiously cursing, and was escorted out of the room by Lord Landsdowne.

After my display of swashbuckling, the least I expected was a round of applause, but all I heard was John's plaintive voice crying: "Would someone please tell me what in heaven's name this was about?"

Mycroft Holmes took the stage. "Of course, doctor. We had received intelligence from our agents abroad that a German spy whose mission was to scuttle the European peace pact had gained close access to His Majesty. We had a very good idea who it was and an even better idea how she would accomplish her mission. If the King were to die, so would the entente cordiale. Since we had no actual proof to back up our suspicion we could not arrest Mademoiselle Perrault. Such an act without the proper evidence could have resulted in an international incident with France, which would have jeopardized the entente. So you see the dilemma that faced us. It was finally decided to create a situation that would encourage her to take action. Earlier, Mrs. Watson, you charged me with being the instigator of this plan, but it was actually Sherlock who plotted out our little drama, which was predicated upon the assumption that Mademoiselle Perrault would be unable to resist taking advantage of our plan to make the King ill. We went so far as to provide her the opportunity by enlisting His Majesty's nine-year-old grandson to plant the firecracker. Needless to say, Sherlock did not actually inject His Majesty, but merely pretended to, catching the solution in a concealed sponge."

John frowned. "But wait a minute, that means that you had to know in advance that I would refuse to administer the dose," he said.

Now Sherlock Holmes spoke up. "You should know by now that I never sit down to a chess board without knowing in advance what moves my opponent will make. Your actions in particular, Watson, are as predictable as the tide."

"Really, Holmes, you make me sound like a trained dog," John complained (and about time!).

"I believe what my brother means, Dr. Watson," Mycroft interjected, "is that while we could not script your role to the extent we had for the dramatis personae present, we counted on your enviable loyalty to oath and Crown rendering you incapable of going through with our plan."

"Very well," I said, "but why was it vital to involve John in this matter at all? Sir Francis could have done it equally well."

"I am afraid it was necessary for the layering of the plot," Mycroft answered. "The success of our plan turned upon Mademoiselle Perrault's feeling secure in her deception every step of the way. Sir Francis Lacking is an important man in the palace, whose reputation is unimpeachable. He could not be brought down easily on charges of incompetence."

"Whereas a humble private doctor could," John said glumly.

"Look at it this way, old boy," Sir Francis added, "a second opinion is always desirable. My role in this was to verify, as another medical man, that the Perrault woman's plan had worked, or at least seemed to. But to make the mademoiselle secure enough in her success to walk into the trap, we had to produce someone expendable to take the blame."

"Expendable!" I shouted.

"What Sir Francis undoubtedly meant was someone who gave the illusion of being expendable," Mycroft said soothingly.

"Well, Mr. Homes," I replied, testily, "I only hope our humble, expendable selves performed our unwitting roles to your satisfaction."

"May I say, madam, that you exceeded our expectations. I doubt any of us could have anticipated your fortuitous skill with a rapier."

"Indeed!" the King cried out, and incredibly, I had all but forgotten his presence. "How can we repay you? A reward? A title perhaps?"

The answer came to me without even thinking. "There is one thing Your Majesty could offer that would satisfy me."

"Name it," he said.

"An apology to my husband, who I fear has been badly used in this affair."

"That is all?" His Majesty asked, and I nodded. "Then by all means! Dr. Watson, you have earned the profound thanks of the Crown, as well as our profound apology for any discomfort we have caused you."

"Your Majesty, I —" John began, but Mycroft interrupted him. "Indeed, Dr. Watson, on behalf of the British government, I am truly sorry for what we have, by necessity, put you through, and offer my hand in friendship."

"And I, sir," added Lieutenant Breakstone, after which Sir Francis Lacking took John's hand and offered his apology. But after that there was a distinct silence. "Well, Mr. Holmes?" I said.

Sherlock Holmes stiffened. "Watson knows of my feelings for him."

"I wish to hear you apologize," I said.

"Yes, Holmes, be about it and let us get down to dinner," His Majesty commanded.

After shooting me a murderous look, Sherlock Holmes faced John and quietly said through clenched jaws, "I am sorry, Watson."

I was satisfied.

On our way back down to the ballroom, John whispered into my ear: "By the way, where did you learn your prowess with a sword?"

"I will tell you later, darling," I answered, then stepped away from him to pull aside Mycroft Holmes. "Mr. Holmes, there is something yet bothering me," I said. "When you first telephoned us you asked that I send away our maid before your arrival. How did you know we had a servant named Missy?"

"My dear Mrs. Watson, His Majesty depends upon my knowing things. I would not be overstating the matter to say that it is indeed my job." Then after giving me a stiff approximation of a bow, Mycroft Holmes lumbered on inexorably towards the waiting banquet table.

THE ADVENTURE OF
THE BRAMLEY COURT DEVIL

"John, I would like to trade seats," I informed my husband, hoping to escape, or at least diminish through distance, the highly annoying snorting sound that was coming from the elderly man seated at my right.

"As you wish, Amelia," John replied, rising and allowing me to inch past until we had exchanged places, though it quickly became evident that not even objectionable sounds would ruin his enjoyment of the evening, which was the first he had taken away from his writing desk in Heaven knew how long. I, however, was feeling less expansive, since the accomplishment of having pulled him away from the recording of his exploits with Sherlock Holmes had been tempered by his insistence on choosing the play we would attend. That, in short, is why we were squeezed into a capacity-filled house at the Monarch Theatre, waiting for the curtain to rise on a penny-dreadful melodrama titled "The Torments of Honoria," rather than seated in the newly opened New Gaiety Theatre, eagerly anticipating its premiere presentation, "The Orchid," which had been my recommendation.

As it turned out, Honoria was not to be alone in torment. I too was suffering at the hands of the playwright, whose cliched and hackneyed dialogue was delivered by the actors with a note of apology in their voices. John, on the other hand, sat raptly through every painful line and absurd convolution of the plot, so much so that I finally abandoned the play entirely and began to watch his reactions, which were far more entertaining.

But my attention was ultimately forced back to the action on stage by the sound of a fearsome shriek, followed by a collective gasp from the cast. I watched with new interest as the actors, moving as one, stepped back to allow a strange, dishevelled man to stagger centre stage. "The devil!" he cried, a look of abject horror on his face, "I seen the Devil in Bramley Court!" The man then collapsed onto the stage and lay still. The actors looked back and forth at one another, vainly trying to figure out what to do, and within seconds, the curtain rapidly descended.

A low murmur rippled through the audience, most of whom, like myself, had obviously realized that something was dreadfully wrong, though a smattering of applause was offered by those who had not. My husband, alas, was in the latter grouping.

"Ripping!" he declared, clapping enthusiastically. "What a way to end an act! It is a mark of a skilled author to concoct such a singular surprise."

"I have a feeling that even the author might be shocked by this turn of events," I replied.

"Really, Amelia, you cannot mean to say that you believe this man was not somehow part of the drama," he protested. But before we could debate the issue further, a lone figure had appeared on stage in front of the curtain, his hands raised in an appeal for silence, which he quickly got.

"Is there a doctor present?" the man called out in a thin, reedy voice.

"Great Scott," John muttered, then leapt to his feet, shouting, "Yes, I am a doctor!" Squeezing past the other theatre-goers to get to the aisle, he dashed to the stage, while I followed as rapidly as my dress would allow. "I am Dr. John H. Watson," he told the man on stage, who in turn identified himself as the stage manager. "And I am Mrs. Watson, here to assist my husband," I hastened to add, and we were quickly ushered through the curtain.

Breathing in the unique aromas of stage paint and makeup, I was suddenly transported back to a wonderful time, long since passed, when I was an actress (albeit an amateur one). I probably would have stood transfixed indefinitely had not the voice stage manager whinnied: "Is he all right?" I then became aware that John was kneeling down beside the prone figure, a red-faced, middle-aged man whose clothing betrayed signs of overuse. After checking the man's pulse at the neck and then the wrist, John gently lowered the limp hand to the floor. His expression told all. "This man is dead," he said.

"Dead?" the stage manager croaked. "How?"

"Difficult to tell," John responded. "I can find no evidence of injury, though judging from his state when he collapsed, I would say it is possible that he died of fright. Does... did he work here?"

"No, I have never seen him before," the stage manager replied. "The doorman said he rushed in from the street, and before he could be stopped, found his way onto the stage. We have already sent someone to fetch the police. Would you be good enough to stay until they arrive, sir?"

"Of course."

"Thank you. I must go and inform the audience that the performance is cancelled. I doubt any of us are in a state to continue." Wringing his hands, the man disappeared through the curtain to make his announcement, which was greeted with a chorus of groans.

We did not have long to wait for the police. Even before the last patron had filed out of the theatre, a familiar figure in a macintosh and bowler hat appeared backstage. "Why, Dr. Watson," he said, "are you now finding out about crimes before the police? Or are you simply causing them yourself?"

In unison, John and I both said: "Inspector Laurie, how to do you?"

"Ah, Mrs. Watson, you are here as well," the inspector said. "It has been a while."

John regarded us with a quizzical expression. "A while? I was not aware you two even knew each other at all."

"Oh, yes," the inspector went on, "Mrs. Watson and Mr. Holmes were helpful in cracking a case a while back."

"When was this?"

"You were out of town, darling, and... oh, I will explain it later," I said, weakly.

"So, doctor, what have we got here?" the inspector asked, but before John could recount the dead man's dramatic appearance, the harried stage manager had reappeared, saying: "I would like to be able to dismiss the cast, inspector, unless you need them."

Inspector Laurie turned to the actors, who were huddled upstage. "All right, listen up," he commanded, then pointing down at the sprawled figure, asked: "Anyone here ever seen this man before?" Each actor in his or her turn responded in the negative, with the stage manager concluding: "He is not one of us, inspector."

"All right, they can go," Inspector Laurie said. Turning back to John and myself, he added: "I would like to hear more from you two, if you don't mind."

"I wish there were more to report," John said. "At one point in the play the man dashed on stage — "

"To the obvious consternation of the actors," I interjected.

" — And shouted something about having seen the devil, then fell down dead."

"The devil, you say?" the inspector said.

"On my honour," John replied.

"No, what I mean is, you're sure he said 'the devil?'"

"I believe his exact words were, 'I seen the devil in Bramley Court,'" I said. Immediately the inspector's face darkened.

John, however, seemed oblivious to this sudden change of mood. "If you ask me, this is an open-and-shut case," he stated.

"Indeed, doctor?"

"Absolutely. Given the facts as we now, I think I can deduce what happened. By the condition of this clothing, which can best be described as shabby, we can deduce that this fellow is of limited means. The redness and slight swelling around his nose reveals him also to have been a heavy drinker, and therefore probably not a man who looked after his health. It is safe to assume that he could have had a serious heart condition and not even known it. This evening, he must have drunk enough to bring on some form of the *delirium tremens*, which in his mind manifested into the appearance of the Devil himself. Panicked, he ran through the streets screaming blue murder, and into the first open door he came upon, which would have been the backstage entrance of this theatre. He staggered out on stage, his mind further confused by the lights and the sudden appearance of an audience, and made his dramatic statement, then expired."

"A very interesting theory, doctor," Inspector Laurie said. "However, that does little to explain the four other people who reported seeing a demon of some sort in the area of Bramley Court over the past three nights."

A half-hour later the three of us sat ensconced in a booth at Simpson's in the Strand, where Inspector Laurie, having confessed to working through supper, was devouring a plate of pork loin and roasted potatoes.

"You don't really believe the devil has arisen in London, do you, inspector?" I asked.

"I'm but a simple policeman, Mrs. Watson, not a theologian," he replied. "But at this moment, I'm not sure what I believe."

"Perhaps you should seek Holmes' opinion of this business," John suggested.

"Aye, and so I tried. I called on him yesterday morning, but his landlady said that he is off somewhere on a case."

This news brought a frown to John's face. "That's odd, Holmes usually notifies me when he is leaving town." I suspect that I may have had something to do with the great detective's sudden coolness toward his bosom friend, since the last time I had seen Mr. Holmes, I had managed to cause him some considerable discomfort in front of the most illustrious witness in the Empire. Deservedly so, I might add. But that was no reason to punish my husband. "Do not worry yourself, darling," I said, " you know Mr. Holmes and his whims better than anyone."

"Yes, I suppose so," he replied. "But in his absence, Inspector Laurie, perhaps I could help you."

The inspector looked from his plate. "Help me what?"

"Help you investigate this singular mystery."

Dabbing at his mouth with a napkin, the inspector said, "Look, Dr. Watson, it's not that I don't value your advice, but I'm hardly in a position to let an amateur get involved the case."

"Amateur?" John bristled. "Really, inspector, I have been called in to assist the police on many occasions."

"Darling, even Mr. Holmes is an amateur, by his own admission," I said. "Besides, the police are paid to look for demons in dark alleys."

"True enough," Inspector Laurie said, "and there are few places in London as dark as Bramley Court. It's the centre of a tight, dirty little maze of narrow alleyways, the perfect hiding place for a criminal on the run. They can't demolish the place fast enough for my liking."

"Demolish it?" I said.

"Aye, as part of the Kingsway improvements. A few years back they cleared out the Clare Market slum to make room for the new thoroughfare between High Holborn and the Strand."

"Yes, I remember," John said, nodding.

"Yet some reason they left Bramley Court, the worst part of the district, standing. I suppose Her Majesty's Government had its reasons. Maybe they didn't need the land yet, or some such. But whatever the reasoning behind it, it is coming down now, and I say good riddance." Inspector Laurie drained the remainder of his coffee cup then dug a shilling out of his pocket and plunked it on the table. "Well, I had better get back to see what the lads have discovered. If you do happen to hear from Mr. Holmes, let me know." He then rose, jammed his bowler back on his head, bid us good evening and took his leave.

John spoke no more about the bizarre occurrence in the theatre, either in the restaurant or on the way home, which was not an encouraging sign. I have known my husband long enough to know that when he does not speak, he is ruminating, and such ruminations too often lead to his taking rash action. My feelings of apprehension were heightened when the yellow glare of the streetlight outside our home in Queen Anne Street revealed that his face had magically shed itself of years, and the distinguished looking grey streaks at his temples had miraculously regained a natural brown hue — a remarkable transformation that occurred whenever my husband was excited by the prospect of a case. But with Mr. Holmes out of the picture (or perhaps *because* of that), I knew that he was contemplating striking out on his own, despite the admonition from Inspector Laurie. My role in this scenario was becoming clear: whatever it took, I must keep him out of harm's way.

I said nothing until the proper moment, which came shortly after the church tower had tolled eleven. Still dressed, John took up his hat and coat once more and announced, "I do not feel sleepy, my dear, I believe I will go out and walk for a bit."

"What a delightful idea," I countered, reaching likewise for my hat and quickly pinning it on. "I shall accompany you."

"Uh, no, there is no reason for that," he replied. "I mean, there is no reason for you to tire yourself."

"Oh, I am not tired either," I lied, "and you know how much I enjoy dank, foggy nights."

For several moments we stood facing each other like fighters in a ring, each knowing exactly what the other one was plotting. Finally John said: "You know, Amelia, that you cannot stop me from going to Bramley Court."

"I am quite aware of that, dear, just as you must be aware that you cannot stop me from accompanying you. Having settled that, shall we go?"

As we sped through the night streets of London in a chilly hansom cab, I startled myself with the realization that, far from preventing my husband from carrying out a rash and possibly dangerous act, I was actually looking forward to approaching the precipice with him. I wanted to know what lie behind the stories of the Bramley Court Devil, and the thought of poking around until I found out gave me a slight tingle of pleasure. Heavens, what on earth had happened to the staid, respectable doctor's wife I used to greet each morning in the mirror? I tried to contain my growing excitement lest John discover it, at which point all would be lost.

Before long we arrived at Holofernes Street, a dark, eerily lifeless passageway that, according to our driver, was the entrance to the district. It quickly became clear that it was also as far into the slum as he would take his steed. The street was dotted with piles of earth and broken stone that spoke of the demolition that had already begun. Inspector Laurie had not been exaggerating in likening the quarter to a maze, and as we proceeded through it, a thick, yellow fog began to envelop us, making it even more difficult to find our way through the web of ancient courts. My squirrel coat was little protection against the night chill, which, along with the bleak setting, sent a shiver through me. "Perhaps this was not a good idea," I offered.

"Perhaps you are right," John answered. "The fog has become so dense there is little we can see. Let us go back home."

But then a third voice, coming from behind us, shattered the quiet. "I thought I had made it clear that this was no place to be at night," it declared. John quickly spun around, taking me with him, and with some effort I was able to make out the form of Inspector Laurie, flanked on either side by a constable. "Mind telling me what you two are doing here?" he asked.

"Simply taking a walk," John said brightly, as though our presence in this dismal quarter was a commonplace occurrence.

"Of course," the inspector said, skeptically.

"But since we are here," I added, through chattering teeth, "have you learned anything more about the man in the theatre?"

The policeman sighed. "I suppose it won't hurt to tell you. Seems his name was Muggerage, at least that's what was written on the inner band of his hat. He most likely lived around here since he frequented a local gin shop over on Great Wild Street. According to the other pub flies he was a quiet sort, stayed pretty much to himself, particularly after his wife disappeared."

"Disappeared?" I said.

"Run off with a sailor, so the gossip goes."

"Anything else you can tell us?" John asked, in tones that sounded so much like those of Sherlock Holmes that I did not know whether to laugh or cry.

The inspector did not reply, his attention focused instead on the sound of running footsteps, which appeared to be coming toward us. "Who's there?" he called out, and soon the figure of a very young constable appeared out of the fog. "Oh, it's you, Bingham. What have you got?"

"'E's gone, sir!" the young constable blurted out."

"Who is gone, constable?"

"The dead man, sir."

"*What*?"

"We called for the wagon, just like you said, but when we went back into the theatre to get him, he was gone."

"Don't tell me you left the body alone!"

"Well, sir, I... that is... all of us reckoned that he was not in so much of a hurry to go somewhere that we could not leave him where he was for a second or two."

"In other words, long enough for someone to slip in and

remove the body right out from under your noses."

"Yes sir," the young constable said, bleakly. "What should we do now, sir?"

"Search the area, man, look for anyone who appears to be carrying a large object. If you see two people together, stop them just as a matter of course. I want the body found, constable!"

"Yes sir!" The younger policeman then disappeared into the yellow mist.

After instructing the two constables who were accompanying him to join in the search, Inspector Laurie turned to John and I. "As for you two, I trust I can rely on your silence regarding this. It's bad enough that the papers are going to get wind of this devils' business, but I don't need them to start trumpeting the notion that an eyewitness rose from the dead and walked away."

"You may be assured, Inspector, that I have no interest in providing the newspapers with sensational information," John said. "However, if a reporter were to approach me directly with a question relating to the rumoured disappearance of this Muggerage, it would hardly feel right to lie about it. Unless... "

"Unless what, doctor?" the Inspector inquired, so tensely that I feared John had overstepped his bounds.

"Unless we were to be taken into your full confidence regarding this case and allowed to see it through to its conclusion."

Inspector Laurie sighed deeply. "All right. Given this turn of events I suppose it won't really hurt to have another brain involved. But mind you, this is strictly unofficial."

After receiving our assurances of cooperation, the inspector released one of the constables to escort us out of the maze and stand watch over us until we were safely inside a cab headed for home. Given the evening's excitement, I had no difficulty sleeping that night. When I arose the next morning, I found that John was already dressed and filling the day room with pipe smoke, and pacing in a circle while pondering the problem. The copies of the *Times*, the *Sphere*, the *Graphic*, the *Illustrated London News* and the Police Gazette that were spread across the table top gave evidence to his having gone out while I slept. True to the Inspector's predictions, the morning papers were, in a matter of speaking, full of the devil.

"Have you arrived at any deductions, darling?" I asked, fanning my way through the smoke.

"Only that this entire matter is most puzzling," he said, stopping his pacing and facing me. "The problem I am having, Amelia, is in trying to decide whether this is simply a case of natural death with bizarre overtones, or cold-blooded murder."

"Heavens, what makes you suspect murder?"

"The disappearance of the body. Why else would it have been taken before it could be thoroughly examined if not to cover evidence of foul play?"

"I cannot imagine. Unless, of course, this Muggerage had something valuable on his person."

John nodded. "That had crossed my mind as well, but if that were the case, why steal the entire body? I confess, Amelia, that I am absolutely confounded. There are enough strange occurrences to fill three such cases, and yet no clues! At least none that I took the time to search for. I could positively kick myself for not examining the body more closely while I had the chance. His clothes, even his shoes, might have revealed something."

"Darling, I doubt even the man's shoes would have given up the secret of the apparition in Clare Market. Unless... "

"Unless what?"

"Unless he sold his soles to the devil," I said, unable to stifle a schoolgirl giggle. Alas, John was not in the mood for levity, and soon left for his surgery. After finishing my toilette, breakfasting, and giving Missy, our maid, her instructions for the day, I departed for the Monarch Theatre, in hopes of obtaining a refund on the price of our tickets for the abortive performance of "The Torments of Honoria."

I managed to arrive at the theatre before the box office had opened, and having nothing better to do, I strolled along its portico, watching the comings and goings of the citizenry of London. My attention was soon focused upon one man who appeared to be running across the green toward the theatre. Pulling a note pad and pencil from his coat pocket, he dashed up the steps, and darted inside. Curious, I followed him and soon found myself as one of an assembly of people gathered in the lobby. Everyone but I was scribbling on a pad — reporters, undoubtedly — and the focus of their attention was none other than "Honoria" herself, now out of costume and makeup (and I hope no one will think it mere *meowing* if I report that this "ingenue" will never see forty again).

"It was the most dreadful experience," she cried, dramatically, "I fear I shall faint once more at the memory of it! He charged onto our stage like a madman, shrieking as though the harpies themselves were in pursuit, made his ghastly declaration, then... fell. Save for the cry of the Congolese Wild Man I once encountered at the circus, I have never heard such a sound emerge from a human being." And so it went, until I decided I had had enough of these fevered histrionics and slipped back through the door.

Once I had finally obtained my refund, I decided to spend the afternoon shopping, or at least walking idly from one store-front to the next, while continuing to turn over in my mind the particulars of this puzzling case in my mind. After a time, though, my mind was as weary as my feet, and being nearly four o'clock, I decided to stop at Buszard's and treat myself to a pot of tea and a scone, after which I hired a cab to take me home.

Much to my surprise I found that John had already re-turned from his surgery and was pouring over a new collection of newspapers. "Oh, there you are, my dear," he said, absently. "I had no appointments this afternoon, so I took the opportunity to leave early."

"Is the devil still front page news?" I asked, slipping off my shoes.

"Even more so. Listen to this: 'Stories of the horrible ap-parition that has become known as the Bramley Court Devil have spread so rapidly that many members of a crew working to widen the road through the area have refused to return to work.' Inspec-tor Laurie will not be pleased to hear that." He read in silence for a few more moments, then exclaimed, "Great Scott, listen to this: 'Miss Evangeline Currey, who claims to have seen the devil Thurs-day night, while walking to her home, describes the creature as standing eight feet tall, bearing the head of a goat, from whose mouth emanated flames.'"

"Good heavens!"

"It certainly sounds fearsome, though I think we can al-low for some exaggeration, if not outright delusion." Picking up the latest edition of the Times from the top of the stack, John glanced down its front page, before settling on a column near the bottom. "Ah, here is yet another eyewitness account," he said. "'Mr. Battison informed the Metropolitan Police of seeing a creature some eight feet in height, with the head of a goat and fire spewing from its —' Good Lord, the descriptions are identical!"

"What does that mean, John?" I asked.

"It means that we can no longer hide behind the notion of delusions. Something is really out there, Amelia, but what? What on earth could possibly fit this description? Certainly not a man. No man stands eight feet tall."

At that moment Missy entered the room to ask: "Will you be taking dinner in this evening, sir? Mum?"

"Yes, though later, Missy, I am not much hungry now," I replied.

"You are not feeling ill, are you?" asked John, ever the

concerned physician.

"I am fine, but I stopped at a tea shop near Oxford Circus while I was out, so — " I stopped suddenly and placed a hand to my forehead. "Oh!"

"What is it, Amelia? Something has come to you, hasn't it?"

"I think I know what kind of man stands eight feet tall and breathes fire," I said. "But how can it be? Missy, please leave us now." Once she had exited the room I told John of my suspicions, tenuous and improbable though they were; nay, *impossible*, since my theory had in it a flaw so enormous as to virtually negate it. But with growing excitement, John theorized a solution of his own that completely eradicated the flaw. "We must contact Inspector Laurie at once!" he cried.

"Indeed, John," I said, "and then we must return to Clare Market and do whatever it takes to raise the Devil."

The sky was darkening by the time we reached Holofernes Street, the unearthly quiet of the now empty neighbourhood was disturbed only by the sounds made by John, myself, Inspector Laurie, and the small army of policemen he had assembled.

"For the time being I will accept your theory as a possibility, Mrs. Watson," the inspector was saying, "but only as a possibility, and a slim one at that. And only because we do not have any better — "

"Shhh, inspector, listen," I interrupted, suddenly aware of a strange noise. "Do you hear that?" From somewhere was coming a muffled thump was followed by a scraping sound, then the thump again, then the scraping, over and over.

"I hear it, too," John said, "it sounds like someone digging with a pickaxe."

"It seems to be coming from over there, perhaps from inside that house," I said. Slowly, we advanced on a dark, dilapidated building that, except for the noise that was indeed originating inside, appeared to be deserted. Inspector Laurie silently motioned for his force to surround the house, and a half-dozen hardy souls proceeded down the foreboding alley that bordered the hovel. Once they were in place, he marched to the front door and pounded on it. "Open this door by order of Scotland Yard!"

The digging sound stopped immediately.

"Whoever is in there, I order you to come out!" the Inspector shouted again, and after a suitable period of silence, cried: "Very well, we are coming in!" Two brawny constables threw themselves against the front door, which proved to be stronger than it looked. They were still at it when the first shouts came from the back of the house. "Mary, Mother of God!" cried one policeman as he ran past us and down the court.

"I believe we have succeeded," I said, trying to sound calm, but it still took all my nerve to face the ghastly apparition that now lumbered down the alley. The eyewitnesses' descriptions were horribly accurate: the top of the goat-thing's head stood even with the roof of the house, and a flare of yellow fire was indeed spurting from its mouth. Its body was obscured by a billowing black drape that glistened in the light of the fire.

"Good Lord!" Inspector Laurie cried, as John simply stood gaping at the thing. I, however, sprang into action.

"Amelia, let the police handle it!" John shouted as I charged the demon, running headlong into its black garment, groping blindly for the plank of wood I felt certain would be there. It was buried within the black cloth, but once I had located it I grasped it tightly with both hands and pushed as hard as I could. With an angry bellow, the figure toppled forward and landed with a thud. Upon impact, the goat's head flew off and the black drape caught fire, and the man inside it all frantically wrestled his way out of it, then spit a mouthful of oily liquid onto the ground. Leaping to his feet, he looked around for an escape route, but quickly realized he was surrounded. "That was quite a show you put on, sir," Inspector Laurie said, as two constables rushed in to grab the man and hold him fast. "I think some of my men will be having nightmares for the next week."

"D— your lousy peeler's hide," cried Mr. Muggerage, very much alive. "How'd you know it was me?"

"Since that was deduced by Mrs. Watson, I shall let her tell you."

"The person who really deserves the credit is the leading actress at the Monarch Theatre," I began. "In speaking with re-porters, she likened your cry as you ran onto the stage to that of a circus wild man, a remark that lay innocently in my memory until jarred loose by trying to imagine what kind of mortal could stand eight feet tall and breath fire. It was then I was struck by the only possible answer: a man with the skills of a stilt-walker and a fire eater — in other words, a circus or side show performer. Since you had already been linked to that vocation by way of your dramatic cry, you became in my mind the prime suspect. But there was one obvious problem with that theory: you were dead, or so we thought. It was my husband who solved that particular conundrum."

"When Amelia confessed to me her suspicions," John said, "I suddenly recalled a trick my friend Sherlock Holmes learned in Tibet, whereby through deep concentration, he can slow his pulse to the point of imperceptibility. It was reasonable to assume that the same trick, or something like it, could be in the repertoire of a side show performer."

"It also served to explain the disappearance of your body," I continued. "When no one was looking, you simply got up and walked away. The one mystery that remains, Mr. Muggerage, is why you have done all this?"

"You're so bl—y smart, you tell me!" he snarled. "You're just as bad as my wife, you are. It was her what got me sacked from the circus, d— her! And d— you, too, you bl—y b———!"

I confess that his speech shocked me, as it would any lady of refinement, but I was completely unprepared for what happened next. Before any of the policemen could stop him, John rushed the man crying, "How dare you!" and struck him with his fist, knocking the villain unconscious with one blow! I had often heard John speak of a youthful temper — "keeping a bull pup" was his term for it — but I had never before witnessed it.

It had obviously taken Inspector Laurie by surprise as well, since he stood open mouthed for a few moments, then recovered enough to order his men to take the limp figure away. "And this time, don't let him get up and walk away from you," he commanded.

"Inspector, called one constable, who was emerging from the house, "I think you'd better have a look inside." Using police torches, we made our way through the dark, filthy structure until we came upon a sight that filled me with revulsion. Dug into the earth under the floor was a shallow grave containing human bones, loosely laid in a tattered woman's garment. "I have a suspicion that Mrs. Muggerage did not run away with a sailor after all," I said, a lump rising in my throat.

Inspector Laurie knelt down by the grave. "Muggerage must have realized that the workmen who demolished the house would uncover the body as well, so he created the Bramley Court Devil, hoping that the ensuing panic would stop the work, at least long enough for him to remove the evidence himself."

"You almost have to admire the man's inventiveness," John said.

Two nights after the horrible discovery in Bramley Court, we found ourselves once more enjoying the convivial hospitality of Simpson's with Inspector Laurie, a fitting place to bring the investigation that had begun there to a close.

"There is one thing I do not yet understand, inspector," I said. "Why did Muggerage rush on stage that night and then fake his own death?"

"I asked him that very thing myself," Inspector Laurie said, digging into his sherried trifle. "It seems that his first appearances as the devil frightened those who saw them, but they failed to spread the kind of widespread panic he was looking for, chiefly because we managed to keep the reports out of the papers. So he had to go public, so to speak, which he did by bursting into a crowded theatre and planting the rumour of the devil to several hundred people at once. As for his death act, that was simply a means of escaping detection. Even the Yard stops short of questioning dead men."

"Ingenious," John said.

"Aye. His only mistake was in choosing the very theatre you two were attending."

"For that you may solely thank my husband," I said.

"I do have to confess, though, Mrs. Watson, that I was prepared not to believe your theory. Tying it all back to Muggerage, just on the supposition that he was once in the circus, was a mighty leap of logic."

John smiled at this. "As Holmes is fond of saying, when you have eliminated the impossible, the only solution left, no matter how improbable, must be the right one. But I must commend you, inspector, at having wrenched the entire story out of this blighter. He seemed to me to be the uncooperative type."

"Oh, that was no trouble, doctor. We told him that either he talked to us or we'd let you come down and take another poke at him."

Taking up John's hand, which was still red and sore from defending my honour, I batted my eyelashes and twittered, "My knight in shining armour!" in such fashion as would have done Honoria proud.

THE ADVENTURE OF THE RETIRING DETECTIVE

"Good God!" my husband cried, clutching the pages of the evening *Times* so tightly that they threatened to rip.

"What is it, John?" I asked, concerned and a little frightened by the intensity of alarm in his tone.

The look of shock remained on his face as he read from the paper: "'The body of a woman found floating in the Thames near the Hungerford stairs has been conclusively identified as Mrs. Irene Norton, the former Irene Adler of the European operatic stage. The police have ruled the death a suicide.' I cannot believe it!"

"How terrible. Did you know this woman?"

"Only by reputation. Irene Adler was entangled in a singular puzzle some years back involving the King of Bohemia. She was the only woman ever to beat Holmes at his own game and as a result, he became fascinated by her. He always referred to her as *the* woman and kept her picture in a place of honour in his room."

I vaguely recalled hearing some mention of *the* woman in the past, but until then, never knew to whom it was referencing. "I must confess, darling," I said, "that I never pictured Mr. Holmes as one capable of schoolboy crushes."

"Oh, it was hardly that. It was her intellect and spirit he admired. He never expected to see her again; indeed, she had vowed never to return to England. Now this. How perfectly terrible for poor Holmes!"

I might have thought it perhaps a bit more terrible for the victim, but I said nothing. If being the wife of Dr. John H. Watson has taught me anything, it is that his odd friend Sherlock Holmes was always at the top of his consideration.

"The poor fellow must be distraught," John continued. "He might even be tempted back onto the needle. I must away to him at once." Rising from the chair, he rushed to the coat rack by the door.

"Must you go now?" I called after him, but I could see the determination setting in his face and realized there would be no stopping him. "Very well, if you must run out now, I shall accompany you," I said, hastening to get my own coat and hat.

"There is no need for you to go, Amelia," he protested, throwing on his coat.

"While I do not have your experience with Mr. Holmes, John, I have known him long enough to realize that he would reject outright a blatant offer of sympathy and assistance, even from you. However, if we were to both appear at his door, saying that we had been walking in the neighbourhood and decided impulsively to drop in for a friendly visit, he would be less likely to erect a guard around himself."

Grudgingly, John agreed.

The night was chilly and the cab was drafty, but fortunately, Mr. Holmes' refuge in Baker Street was not very far from our own home in Queen Anne Street. "I have this strange sense of foreboding," John confessed as we walked up the familiar stairs to Mr. Holmes' second floor rooms. While I do not know what he was steeling himself for, I can state with certainty that the sight that greeted us at the door came as a shock.

The woman who opened the door to John's former apartment appeared to have just emerged from her bath. Her long, auburn hair was still set and the only covering on her body was a man's dressing gown! The scent of shag tobacco that permeated the garment identified it as belonging to Sherlock Holmes. But what on earth was this wet, unclad woman doing wrapped inside it?

"I... I... I am s-sorry to disturb you," John burbled out, directing his gaze towards his shoes.

"No disturbance at all, Dr. Watson," the woman said, her voice betraying American roots. "Won't you come in?"

John suddenly looked up. "Do we know each other?" he asked, studying the woman's face, which was radiantly beautiful even without any trace of cosmetics. His jaw then dropped as he cried: "Great Scott, you are Irene Adler! I recognize you from that photograph of Holmes's. But the newspapers reported that— "

"Let us discuss it inside, please," she entreated, "the open door is creating quite a draft."

Once we had entered the previously male-only domain, Irene smiled at me and said: "And you must be Amelia, Sherlock told me that Dr. Watson had recently married."

"And where is Mr. Holmes?" I asked, returning the smile.

Michael Mallory

"Sherlock is out, but he mentioned that you would most likely be contacting him as soon as you saw the fraudulent report he planted in the newspapers. Please make yourselves at home, while I go change," she said, exiting into a side room.

"But that is my bedroom," John muttered, his eyes following her through the door.

"*Was* your bedroom, dear," I said, patting his hand.

"Surely she cannot be living here!"

The opportunity to find out came quickly, as Sherlock Holmes breezed through the door a few seconds later. "Ah, Watson, how good to see you," he said perfunctorily, tossing his hat on a battered hat rack in the corner and draping his coat over the back of the settee. "And Mrs. Watson as well," he added, a degree or two more coolly. Then a phantom smile broke across his face. "Your look of Puritanical disapproval, Watson, tells me that you have already encountered Irene. I assure you that the reason for her presence is as simple as it is necessary," Holmes stated, stuffing tobacco into a sooty clay pipe that looked as though it had recently been excavated from a Bronze-age dig. "I desire to keep her alive."

The woman in question returned to the room, dressed now in a simple white shirtwaist and dark grey skirt, her still-damp hair combed down straight and draping her shoulders. I noticed that she wore no rings on her hand, even though she continued to use the name, Mrs. Norton. A widow, I guessed. What I could not discern was why she should be having so many difficulties staying alive as to require the services of a detective.

"Sit down, please," Holmes said, lighting the pipe as he draped his long frame across a battered armchair. "I would offer you coffee, but I have sent Mrs. Hudson away. As startled as you seemed to be by Irene's presence, Watson, Mrs. Hudson would have been scandalized to the point of evicting me from the premises. I intend to keep her away until this dark business has been concluded."

"What dark business?" John asked.

"Perhaps I should let Irene herself explain," Holmes said, leaning back and closing his eyes while the pipe continued to smolder in his hand.

Mrs. Norton turned to us and began: "My husband, Godfrey, died two years ago. He was, as you may recall, Dr. Watson, a lawyer. After a number of years on the continent we resettled in America, where Godfrey quickly became one of Boston's most successful attorneys, catering mostly to the crème of New England society. But being a foreigner on American shores himself, he was rarely able to refuse an appeal for help from another foreigner, even if they possessed no resources to pay him. It was through one such case that we first learned the truth about Randolph Harding Bowers."

"Who is Randolph Harding Bowers?" I inquired.

"I am sorry, I had forgotten that the name means little in England," she replied. "In the United States, however, he is as well known as T.R. himself."

I looked to John, still puzzled. "T.R.?" I wondered aloud.

"Theodore Roosevelt, the American president," Holmes interjected, the first indication that he had remained awake since Mrs. Norton began speaking.

"To directly answer your question, Mrs. Watson," Irene Norton said, "Randolph Harding Bowers is a man of almost incalculable wealth and power, he either owns or is partnered in a good many of the nation's mining and manufacturing companies. It was one of his factory employees who contacted Godfrey, seeking his help, and after hearing the man's strange story, Godfrey began an investigation of his own, speaking with other workers in Bowers' factories and mines. Not only were these interviews done at his own expense, but were accomplished with a secrecy and cunning that would have done Sherlock proud."

Sherlock. That was the third time the woman had regarded Mr. Holmes in a very familiar fashion, and I began to wonder anew about her presence in his rooms in a state of undress, only to push the thought out of my mind as too immoderate to contemplate.

Mrs. Norton continued: "Over the period of one year, Godfrey had spoken with dozens of Bowers workers, men and women, and in every case had received the exact same story: Randolph Harding Bowers was not an employer in any accepted sense of the word, but rather a slave-holder."

"A slave-holder?" I cried. "I thought that sort of thing had been abolished years ago."

"Indeed it was," she replied. "Unfortunately, Randolph Bowers is not a man to let the law stand in his way. Using a series of agents placed throughout Europe, Asia and Australia, Bowers would find people who desired to immigrate to America and offer them transport, lodging and a job once they had arrived. Most of these unfortunates told Godfrey that it sounded like a dream come true. But once the would-be immigrants arrived in America, secretly, via a shipping line owned by a friend and confederate of Bowers', they were immediately put to work in a Bowers mine or a Bowers factory and were provided with a filthy cot in an overcrowded bunkhouse and meagre board in lieu of wages."

"The unmitigated villain," John huffed. "Did not anyone

object?"

"If anyone tried, they were threatened with deportment to lands other than their own. If anyone talked of escape, they were detained in one of Bowers's makeshift jails. If anyone actually tried to escape, they would invariably be caught and..."

"Go on," John said.

"...And their bodies would be placed on public display as an example to the others."

"Good God!"

"Was this man Bowers responsible for your husband's death as well, Mrs. Norton?" I asked.

"Please call me Irene," she responded with a smile, which I returned. "And no, he was not. During the year in which he was investigating Bowers, Godfrey began to take ill. He tried to hide his condition from me, but it soon became painfully clear that he would be denied the time to use the evidence he had uncovered to fight this dangerous man. On his deathbed, Godfrey handed me his notebook, containing notes of all the interviews he had conducted as well as the names of the other wealthy businessmen involved in the scheme. My last words to my husband were that I would somehow find a way to bring Randolph Harding Bowers down. Now, of course, it has become all the more imperative."

"Why is that?"

"Bowers has announced his plans to run for the Governorship of Massachusetts, the avowed first step in his quest for the Presidency itself. Through his network of spies, he has managed to find out about Godfrey's investigation and he knows that I am holding the evidence that would ruin him. In short, Mrs. Watson... Amelia... he is on to me. I know for a fact that I have been followed for the past three months."

"Cannot you go to the American authorities with your evidence?" John asked.

"Powerful men tend to have powerful friends, Dr. Watson," Irene replied. "I honestly do not know whom I can trust. But my immediate problem is that I cannot at this moment lay my hands on the notebook. Godfrey's final instructions were to send it to an old friend of his, Simon Belfont, here in London, with the instructions that the notebook be deposited into a private bank vault, and the key be sent back to me in Boston. He felt it would be safer if the notebook was in a different country, out of Bowers' reach. Unfortunately, I fear he underestimated the length of the man's arms. Once I realized that I was being watched, my only thought was to retrieve the notebook, my only true weapon against Bowers and his army of thugs, as soon as possible. I booked passage to

England under an assumed name, hoping to be out of the country before my actions were discovered. Alas, I was not successful."

"Which is why Holmes planted the suicide notice in the papers," John said.

"Precisely, Watson," Holmes said, suddenly bolting upright in his chair, "and with the complete approval of Scotland Yard, I might add. If Irene's pursuers believe that she has been driven to take her own life, their own investigation will be rerouted, and that will allow us enough time to overcome the major obstacle in this case."

"Which is...?" John asked.

"Finding the notebook, of course."

I was becoming confused, which was not an uncommon occurrence in the presence of Mr. Holmes. "But didn't you just say the notebook in the bank vault?" I queried.

"Indeed I did," Irene replied, "and so indeed I thought it was. But when I went around first thing this morning and offered my identification as well as the key, the vault proved to be empty. The notebook is missing."

"But surely this can lead to only one conclusion," John cried. "The fellow to whom you sent the notebook never put it in the vault."

"*Of course* that is the only conclusion, Watson, a child of seven could see that!" Mr. Holmes said brusquely, and again I wondered how John had managed to endure his friend's condescension for so many years. "The bigger problem," the detective went on, "is that Simon Belfont appears to have disappeared as well."

"What is to be done, then?" John asked.

Pacing back and forth and puffing smoke like a nervous locomotive, the detective replied: "First: Mrs. Watson, I must ask you to take Irene in as a boarder for the time being. She will be safer there than here."

I looked to John, whose expression indicated total agreement and willingness, before answering, "Very well. Missy, our maid, is away visiting family, so Irene can have in her room."

"It is settled then," Mr. Holmes said. "As for you, Watson, I will require you to be here at Baker Street."

"I am at your call, Holmes," John said, and I opened my mouth to protest, but shut it again, knowing that when he was on a case, nothing on earth that would stop him. Least of all me.

"Now, Watson," Mr. Holmes went on, "please remove your hat and coat and give them to Irene, so that anyone who might be watching from outside will see Dr. and Mrs. John H. Watson leave, the same as they arrived."

"But if someone really is watching, don't you think they will be able to tell the different between Irene in an overcoat and my husband?" I protested.

"Not if the two of you call upon the acting skill I know you both to possess in order to fool them," Holmes said, permitting himself a smile. "You must go now. Watson and I have a great deal of work to do."

"Be careful," I begged my husband, and was surprised to hear Irene bid the same to Sherlock Holmes.

Clad in John's coat and hat, and walking with robust movements, Irene Norton presented a much better image of a man than I would have suspected possible. The biggest problem in the deception was the fact that she stood several inches shorter than my husband. But reaching up on her tiptoes, while I crouched as low as I possibly could and still maintain a normal appearance. We stood in the doorway to 221b until a cab appeared within hailing distance, which Irene signalled. When it stopped, I put my arm through hers, as I normally would my husband's, and together we entered the cab.

Once we were on our way, Irene appeared to relax. "I truly appreciate your help, Amelia," she said.

"It seems little enough," I replied, "if this man Bowers is really that dangerous."

"If not stopped, I believe Randolph Harding Bowers could become the most dangerous man in the world. But if anyone can thwart him, it is Sherlock."

"You know, Irene, it has struck me that you always call Mr. Holmes by his Christian name."

"A display of comfortable familiarity about which you are curious?" she replied, a wry smile on her face.

"Guilty, m'lud," I answered, which made her laugh.

"Perhaps some day, after we have become better friends, I will tell you all about it."

The cab soon pulled up to the kerb in front of our house in Queen Anne street, which, after paying the driver, we quickly entered. Once inside, however, I stopped, suddenly alarmed.

"What is it?" whispered Irene, seeming to sense my concern.

"The lamp in the sitting room has been turned off," I whispered back. "I know we left it on. Someone has been here." It was then I heard a muffled thump coming from somewhere inside our home. "They are still here!" I shouted, grabbing Irene's arm and wrenching the door open. "We must get out!"

But the next sound I heard caused me to stop, and I turned back as the weak, pain-filled voice called: "Dr. Watson... is that you?"

"Whoever it is, he sounds injured," Irene said.

"Let us go see, then, " I said, withdrawing the sturdiest of John's walking sticks from the umbrella stand and holding it in front of me as a weapon as we entered the sitting room. In the darkness I was able to make out a shape sitting in John's chair. "Do not move, I am armed," I told the shape, as I made my way to the lamp, clicking it on. As soon as the room was illuminated, the man in the chair cried: "For God's sake, turn it off! The light... like daggers in my eyes!" I gasped at the terrible sight of the strange man, whose bearing was hardly that of a ruffian, but whose face was covered in bruises, one of which all but closed his right eye. I switched the lamp off, casting the room once more into darkness.

"Who are you?" I asked.

"My name is Belfont, Simon Belfont," he muttered, then turned in the direction of Irene. "Are you Dr. Watson?"

"No, I am Irene Norton, Godfrey's wife," she replied, throwing off John's coat and hat.

"Oh God," he moaned, "it's because of you that I've been held captive and tortured."

"Tortured?" I cried.

"Being bound... blindfolded... beaten... in my book, that is torture." The poor man actually produced a small, sardonic laugh as he added: "But it was not my book that the men wanted, was it?"

Irene suddenly became alarmed. "The notebook — you haven't given it to them, have you?"

"No. It is in a safe place. For now, at any rate."

"Please, tell me everything," Irene beseeched.

"Yes, including how you ended up in my sitting room," I added.

"In a way, I have no one to blame but myself," Belfont began, his voice now somewhat stronger, but still laboured. "About a week back I noticed an ad in the "agony" columns of the *Times*, which read: 'Mrs. G. Norton, recently returned from America, seeks what she has lost. Come in person,' and then it gave an address."

"I put no such ad in the papers!" said Irene.

"I know that now," Belfont continued. "The address in question turned out to be a vacant building, so I turned around and came back. Only later did I realize that the summons was a trap, and that the empty building was being watched for whomever might turn up. From that moment on I was aware of someone following me, watching me. I saw the man repeatedly on the street. He was not very proficient at his task. I quickly realized that I was not the subject of this bizarre game, but rather Godfrey's notebook, though I was determined not to lead my pursuers directly to it. Fortunately, John Hemmings, the manager of the bank, is also a member of my club. I convinced him to open the vault with the bank's key and deliver the notebook to me, which he did."

"That is why the box was empty when I got there," Irene said.

Simon Belfont nodded. "I had just managed to get it to its hiding place when I was abducted. My watchers must have gotten impatient and decided to take more drastic measures. There were two of them, and they succeeded in beating the information out of me... or so they thought. I told them of the bank vault and added that I did not possess a key, all of which was perfectly true."

"How did you get away?" I asked.

"Like most brutal men, my captors were quite stupid," Belfont replied. "I convinced them that I would act on their behalf and get the key from Mrs. Norton when she arrived. In return, they loosened the rope holding me. Once they had fallen asleep, I worked my way out of my bonds and escaped. My first thought was to go immediately to Baker Street to see Sherlock Holmes. But upon arrival in the cab, I noticed that the same man who had been following me was standing across the street, watching the house. I told the driver that I had changed my mind. It was then that I discovered that cabmen know everything there is to know about London."

"How so?" I inquired.

"The fellow quite frankly informed me that I seemed more in need of a doctor than a detective, and offered to take me to the home of Dr. John Watson, where I would have access to both. So here I came. I apologize for the means of entry," the poor man said, gesturing towards the window, which I only now realized was open, "but no one came to the door."

Irene leaned close to him. "Mr. Belfont, please tell me where you have put the notebook."

My eyes had become accustomed to the darkness, and I was able to make out a tiny, grim smile that cut through the pain etched on the man's face. "The one place too obvious to be considered," he said. "Columns... that is my revenge. I was duped through the agony column. Let us see if they find their way through *my* columns."

"But where, Mr. Belfont, *where*?"

The man's smile quickly dissolved into a grimace of pain,

and he grabbed his head with both hands and moaned, then fell limp.

"We must get him to a hospital," I said. Leaving Irene with the stricken man, I rushed outside to try and find help, which soon arrived in the form of a police constable. I gave him only the barest of facts regarding the presence of a strange, injured man in my sitting room, and before long an entire troupe of policemen arrived at our home. An officer who identified himself as Sergeant Potts supervised the transport of the unconscious Mr. Belfont to nearby Middlesex Hospital. As they were leaving, I asked the sergeant to please contact Sherlock Holmes regarding the matter.

By the time the excitement was over, it was nearly eleven o'clock and I felt exhausted. Irene, however, still looked alert, if somewhat troubled. I practically fell into John's armchair, which still carried the warmth of our unfortunate visitor. "I shall never be able to understand how John thrives on this sort of thing," I muttered.

Irene appeared deep in thought. "What do you suppose he meant by 'columns'?" she asked.

"It sounded like delirium to me."

"True, but the other thing he said, something about hiding the notebook in a place too obvious to be considered, seemed quite lucid."

"Until the poor man recovers, I fear we shall never know what he really meant." I rose from the chair and yawned. "I am sorry, Irene, but I simply must get some sleep. Our maid's room is through there. It is not large but the bed is comfortable and bedding clean."

"Thank you, but I think I will stay up a bit longer."

I could see that finding Simon Belfont, only to have the information he possessed slip away, was greatly troubling Irene, but I was in no condition to sit up with her and keep her company. Upon bidding her goodnight I heading for the bedroom, and minutes later slipped in between the sheets on our bed, which was destined to remain cold and lonely for the rest of the night. The last conscious image my mind produced before surrendering to sleep was that of a row of Ionic columns, a picture planted in my head by the unfortunate Simon Belfont.

It is difficult to say how long I had been asleep prior to bolting upright in the bed, my head spinning, and any hope of further sleep chased away fox pursued by hounds. I dashed out into the sitting room to find Irene, still dressed, asleep on the sofa. I shook her gently. "Irene, wake up."

"Hmmm," he muttered, opening one eye, then another.

"Amelia, what is it?"

"Irene, Mr. Belfont was not delirious," I said. "He was telling us exactly where the notebook is hidden!"

We could not, of course, act upon my intuition at that moment, but after a sleepless, though hardly unpleasant night, given the company, Irene and I set out early the next morning, far too anxious to be tired. Taking the omnibus to Great Russell Street, we were soon standing in front of one of the city's most notable Classical facade. "It is in there, behind the columns," I said, staring at rows of them.

Irene smiled. "The perfect place to hide a book," she said. "Our Mr. Belfont was quite clever."

Without another word, we entered the British Museum and made our way towards the great Library. If my supposition was correct, it would not take long to find the notebook. Rushing to the "N" section, the two of us followed the names printed on the spines of the books until we arrived at one slender volume which had no printing at all.

"Here it is!" Irene cried, only to be *shushed* by a group of readers nearby. Almost reverently, she pulled the treasure from the shelf, where it had been hidden in plain sight. Flipping through the pages drew from her a sigh of relief. "It is all intact, every page," she said. "We must away to Baker Street now."

"No, Irene," I said. "Look over there."

A rough, villainous looking specimen was standing in the entrance way to the Library, regarding us with grim amusement.

"Another one over there," Irene whispered, drawing my attention to yet another man whose gaze never left us. All in all, there were four of them positioned throughout the book-filled rotunda. "God in Heaven!" she cried out, "is there no escape from them?"

The sudden rise in her voice prompted one elderly scholar, who was perusing volumes nearly as dusty as himself, to *ahem* rather pointedly before informing us that "this is a library!" I was about to point out to him the utter redundancy of his statement, when I saw a beatific smile break out on Irene's face.

"A library, sir?" she said demurely, stepping towards him, "I thought it was a concert hall." And with that Irene Norton, *nee* Adler, opened her mouth and produced the most beautiful contralto tones I have ever heard. I then remembered the planted suicide notice John had read, which had named her as a star of the European operatic stage.

What her selection was from I could not say, though it was performed as though she were singing for her life (which, in a sense, she was). While a few of the Library patrons appeared to appreciate the unexpected concert, there were more like the pinched man standing next to us who seemed to list making noise in the British Library as one of the primary qualifications for perdition.

"Please madam," the man shouted, in spite of himself, "be quiet!"

"Oh, be quiet yourself!" I shouted back. "You are interrupting the concert!"

It was not long before the police constables arrived, which I had come to realize was the purpose of Irene's impromptu aria, and as the first policeman strode through the reading tables towards us, she suddenly stopped singing and levelled a finger at one of our burly surveillants, shouting, "There he is, constable, that is the man!" Startled, the man turned and started to dash out, but was stopped by another constable. The others in the Library followed suit, though I am very glad to say that none made it past the line of officers.

Irene and I were, of course, escorted out under police guard as well, and I daresay that we did little to help our cases by giggling like a pair of naughty schoolgirls all the way to Bow Street. By the early afternoon, though, we were released, thanks to the depositions of the men who had been assigned to watch us, the evidence of the notebook and the testimonials on our behalf from John and Mr. Holmes, who had been sent for as soon as we reached the Magistrate's Court. But our freedom was predicated upon the solemn vow that we never again to create a public row in the British Museum.

On the way back to Baker Street, I inquired after the condition of Mr. Belfont.

"He is concussed, though he should recover fully with time," John responded. "In fact, we have hopes he will be well enough within a few days to at least to inform us as to the whereabouts of the notebook."

"The two of you saved us that trouble," said Holmes, whose sphinx-like countenance made it impossible to tell whether he was annoyed by our actions or amused.

John continued: "Once the recovery of the notebook looked imminent, Holmes took the liberty of contacting an American justice official who is at this moment sailing to England in order to receive it in person. He assured us that, based on your husband's testimony, this Bowers fellow is as good as imprisoned."

Upon hearing this, Irene muttered something so quietly that I was unable to distinguish it. At first I though it might have been a prayer, but upon reflection a few days later I realized that it must have been: "I have done it, Godfrey."

By then, though, everything had changed.

The four of us spent the rest of the day together, and it was very strange to see Mr. Holmes in purely social circumstances. He remained quiet, if not boyishly bashful throughout, though I detected enough subtle looks and smiles exchanged between he and Irene to make me wonder anew what had once passed between them that they were not revealing.

It was dusk by the time we returned to Baker Street. We had just exited our cab and watched it pull away from the kerb when the sounds of another approaching carriage filled the street. "Mrs. Norton!" a voice called from behind us, and Irene turned around.

"Irene, no!" shouted Mr. Holmes, and John and I spun around to see a dark brougham with a man leaning from its window. With a lightning-fast snap of his hand the man flung something, though I could not see what it was. The carriage then sped away and disappeared into the night. The next thing I heard was John shouting: "Great God!" and for a moment everything seemed to be happening at once, but slowly. I heard John once more, this time saying: "Irene, do not try to move, we shall get an ambulance," and only then did I see a sight that tore my heart from my body. Irene Norton lay on the sidewalk, her simple dress coloured by her own blood. John was kneeling beside her, his skilled surgeon's hands hovering helplessly over the knife that was embedded in her chest.

"We will get you help," he was saying.

"No, too late," Irene whispered. With obvious pain, she raised her head and looked toward Mr. Holmes, who now knelt beside her as well. "I shall soon see Godfrey," she panted, "and I shall tell him that I saw you again, Sherlock." A slight, knowing smile then graced her lips. "But I shan't tell him everything." Her head fell back down on the sidewalk, and John slowly stood up, removed his coat and draped it over top of her.

Sherlock Holmes slowly rose, his gaze still cast down at the body. When he finally looked up, I saw more pain reflected in his eyes than I believed possible for a man to bear. "I should have foreseen this," he said in a flat, dead voice that caused me to shiver even as I wept. "I swear to you, Irene, that I shall not rest until I have found the man or men responsible for this. This night, Sherlock Holmes shall cease to exist, except to bring this ring of killers to justice. Watson, I shall require your help for this."

"Anything Holmes, anything," John choked.

"As soon as this notebook is handed to the American authorities, I will leave Baker Street. You will inform the public that I am no longer available to act a consulting detective."

"What shall I say?"

"Say anything, Watson. Say I retired to the country to keep bees. I do not care. I leave it in your hands."

"Where will you go, Mr. Holmes?" I asked, sniffing and sobbing like a child.

"Everywhere. Nowhere. Only by becoming a phantom will I be able to track down the devils who have done this."

"We will we see you again, won't we?" John asked, his voice unsteady.

"When the need occurs, yes," Holmes said quietly. "Until then, Watson, goodbye." He turned and stiffly strode to the door of Baker Street, his thin hands clenched into ivory fists. But at the stoop, he turned back. "One more thing you must do, Watson," he called.

"Yes, Holmes."

"You must protect your wife and keep her safe. If you do nothing else, old friend, do that." Sherlock Holmes then entered 221b and closed the door.

I have no doubt that John and I shall indeed see Mr. Holmes again, though when and where I cannot say. Yet whenever I think of him — which is surprisingly often — I find myself hoping that his self-imposed quest will not be a long one, and that he will manage to find peace within himself and return to being the same brilliant, righteous, infuriating, and ultimately all-too-*human* being who, in a strange way, captivated the brave and loyal heart of my husband, Dr. John H. Watson.

And in an even stranger way, captured a little bit of mine as well.

THE ADVENTURE OF THE DISAPPEARING COACH

"Another letter from the doctor, ma'am," Missy, our maid, announced brightly, as she flitted in and dropped the morning mail into my lap.

"Thank you, dear," I muttered, eagerly tearing open the envelope from my husband, who had been gone near a fortnight on a public speaking tour, of all things, and whom I had been missing dreadfully. Unfolding the letter, I read, in familiar handwriting:

> *My dearest Amelia,*
>
> *The reception in Leeds was even greater than that in Sheffield, which, as I mentioned in my last letter, was quite encouraging, to say the least. People everywhere in the Kingdom seem to want to hear first-hand about my dealings with Sherlock Holmes. I am, of course, continuing to spread the news of Holmes' "retirement," as he wished, and I am happy to report that my podium style is improving with each lecture. Those lessons in public speaking technique that you gave me have proven invaluable. On Friday I am off to York, which promises the largest audience yet. There has been talk about expanding the tour to another four cities —*

(Heavens, *another* fortnight spent alone? I would like to give a speech of my own to the booking agent who convinced John to take on this new venture.)

> *— but I have discouraged such talk as I do not wish to tire myself. Neither do I want to spend the better part of the next month away from you, my dear.*

All bitter thoughts were erased by that last sentence. Dear, sweet John! I held the letter close to my heart, a poor substitute for having John home, though oddly comforting in its own way. Soon, however, curiosity about the other envelope Missy had delivered forced me to put aside my thoughts of John. This envelope was also addressed to me, though in a rough hand that I did not recognize. Inside I discovered a ragged piece of card upon which a note was hastily (and not very properly) scrawled:

> Amelia,
> Im in trouble — their holding me at Scotland yard but I didnt do nothing. They dont beleve me. I need your help.
>
> Harry Benbow.

Good heavens, Harry Benbow! What on earth had he gotten himself into this time? Even though we had only recently become reacquainted after an absence of some twenty years, I counted Harry as one of my closest friends. We had acted together with the Delancey Amateur Players when I was little more than a schoolgirl, and while it could be argued that I knew very little of his life since, I certainly knew him well enough to realize that he was no common criminal.

I read over the note again, searching for some indication that it was a product of Harry's characteristic sense of humour, but could discern none. The only clear message was that Harry was in trouble, and it was my duty as his friend to try and help him.

Although the rain had not yet begun to fall, a chilly mist permeated the air as I shivered on top of the bus (for no seats were available below) all the way to the imposing red brick edifice of New Scotland Yard. Marching inside, I requested to speak with a sergeant (or higher-up) and was directed to an overstuffed man with far more hair in his eyebrows than upon his head. "I am Mrs. John H. Watson," I announced, "and I should like to be taken to Harry Benbow, who is falsely being held prisoner here."

The sergeant's bushy brows furrowed as he regarded me, then his face brightened and he said, "Oh, right, Benbow, the suspect in the Radford kidnapping case."

"Kidnapping?" I cried. "That is absurd. If Harry is a kidnapper, I am the Queen of Sheba. Who is in charge of the case? Inspector Laurie?"

"No ma'am, Inspector Carrigan's the man on that one, but if I was you, I wouldn't go sounding off to him. He's not in much of a mood for it, with the newspapers on his back, and all."

Suddenly I made the connection between an article that had appeared in the Times a day or two back and poor Harry's predicament. The article had detailed the disappearance of the two young sons of a wealthy businessman living in Mayfair and the subsequent ransom note, asking for, if memory served, £50,000. "I would be grateful if I could see Inspector Carrigan at once," I said. "It is important."

After being ushered through a seemingly endless maze of desks and offices, I finally arrived at a cramped cubbyhole inhabited by man of dark and rough complexion, who appeared to be asleep in his chair.

"Pardon me, sir," the sergeant said, "but here's a woman who says she has information on the Radford case."

The man opened one eye and regarded me somewhat suspiciously before inflicting daylight upon his other eye. "I suppose you had better tell me then," he grumbled. "Who are you and what do you know?"

"My name is Amelia Watson and I know that you are holding the wrong man as a suspect," I said.

At that Inspector Carrigan broke out with a harsh, snorting laugh that conveyed very little mirth. "Oh, we've got the wrong man, have we? And I suppose that evidence we found on him is the wrong evidence, too."

"What evidence?"

The inspector leaned back in his chair and surveyed me from head to toe and back again, a gesture I find rude and demeaning in the extreme. "Just what is your interest in this case?" he asked.

"I am a friend of Harry Benbow's," I said, coolly. "May I sit down?"

"As you wish," he said, and I took the only seat available in the office.

"Now then, please tell me what evidence you have against Harry."

After taking a pinch of snuff, he began: "Well, it seems the younger of the two boys has this toy, a stuffed bear doll that's called a Neddie, or Teddy, or something like that. It was sent over from the States by some American business partner of Andrew Radford — he's the boys' father — and when the boy disappeared, the doll disappeared, too, which says to us that he must have had it with him. But then up pops this Harry Benbow, and guess what he's holding?"

"The bear?"

"Right. Both Mr. and Mrs. Radford positively identified it. So you tell me: if Benbow isn't the kidnapper, how did he get that toy?"

I had to admit that it did not sound good for Harry. Still, I could not accept that he would have anything to do with such a horrible crime. "May I see Harry?" I asked.

"No, you may not," he answered, with finality.

It was becoming obvious that mere persistence was not going to budge this man, so I decided upon a different, if somewhat shameless tactic. Pulling out my handkerchief, I began to dab at my eyes while sobbing: "Poor Harry, I hate to think of him in that horrible cell, all alone, with no one to talk to."

It took the production of nearly as much rainfall from my eyes as was now pattering into the Thames outside, but eventually Inspector Carrigan relented. "Oh, crikey, go and see him then!" he cried. "Just stop that blubbering!"

"Thank you," I twittered, dashing out of the office before my sobs began to sound too much like stifled laughter.

Minutes later I was being escorted by the sergeant down to a ghastly row of holding cells, so bleak and foreboding, that I shivered as I walked through. We stopped at the very last cell, the door of which was unlocked by the warder. Inside, looking confused and defeated, was the diminutive figure of Harry Benbow.

"Amelia!" he shouted as soon as he saw me, "thank heaven you've come!"

"What have you done now, Harry?" I asked.

"*Gor*, I wish I knew! One minute I'm minding my own business, and in the next I'm being accused o' pinching some Mayfair toff's kiddies! Or maybe I should say his *toff*-spring." He waggled his eyebrows and grinned.

"Don't joke, Harry," I said, laughing in spite of myself. "We have to find a way to get you out of here."

"Right, so here's what we do: you put your friend Sherlock Holmes on the case and he finds the real kidnapper, and I'm out o' here before you can say Bob's your uncle!"

I sighed. "So that was why you wanted me to come. Harry, Mr. Holmes has gone away. He is no longer taking cases. Not even John knows where he is."

Poor Harry had turned pale at the news. "Gone away?" he whimpered.

"I am sorry," I added, helplessly. "But why don't you tell me what happened and maybe I can find some way to help."

"All right. I've told everyone else 'round here, but none o' them believes me. See, for the past month or so I've been doing a little busking, not because I have to, mind you, but just to keep in practice. Anyway, I settled into a spot near the Tower Bridge. There's a good crowd o' people down there and I'm giving 'em some o' the old songs, a few dances, some patter, you know. Then one day, as I'm stepping out for a pint and a bit o' fish, I see this coach come tearing around the corner like the Devil himself was driving it, and coming from inside is the sound of some poor little tyke crying his eyes out. Then I see this thing come flying out the coach window, so I go over to look, and it's this little bear cub toy. I figure the little duck's lost his toy and that's why he's so upset. So I start to run after the coach to return it, and it turns onto a dead end street. But by the time I get there, the coach, horse, and screaming tyke are now all inside some big shed, and as I'm running towards it, the driver closes the doors. Then..."

"Go on, Harry."

"Then I run up to the building but the door's locked from the inside, so I peek inside the window... and there's nothing there, Amelia."

"Nothing?"

"No coach, no horse, no driver, no crying tyke. Nothing."

"Could they have gotten out another way?"

"I would've seen 'em. They just disappeared. So I says to myself, 'Harry, you got two choices: you can go barking just thinking about it, or you can go back to work.' So I go back to work, but now I've got this cute little bear, and I figure I might as well work it into the act. So I start feeding the bear straight lines and throwing my voice into it for the laughs. And it's going great with the crowds. Then one afternoon I see this bobby, and he's getting real interested in the bear. I'm thinking, he likes the jokes, but the next thing I know, there's a whole circle of 'em standing 'round me, and before I know it I'm brought down here and tossed in the clink. This Inspector Carrigan bloke, he just keeps demanding to know where those two boys are hidden, and he won't even listen to my story."

"And he is naturally under pressure to find the missing boys," I muttered. "Harry, I think might be able to get you out of here. It may not work, but it is worth a try." I then called for the warder, who took a leisurely amount of time opening the door, and asked to be taken once more to Inspector Carrigan.

"Well, Mrs. Watson," he said as I re-entered his office, "you seem to have regained your composure. Did you have a nice chat with Benbow?"

"Yes," I said, quietly, "and I feel I owe you an apology."

"Indeed?"

"I did not believe you, but talking with Harry, I came to realize that he must be guilty. I dabbed at my eyes again. "I feel so betrayed. I only wish there was something more I could do to help you."

The inspector leaned across his desk in conspiratorial fashion. "You'd be willing to help us, eh? Do you think he'd tell you where the boys are?"

"I don't know. But listen, I had a thought on the way back here: what if Harry was released and then his movements were tracked? He might lead us straight to the children."

"He might run, too."

"Not with me watching him," I replied. "He trusts me, my presence would not be a threat to him."

"No, it sounds too risky."

"Inspector, think of those two poor boys. What if they have been left alone? What if something dreadful were to happen to them while Harry was being held as a suspect? Think of the public outcry!"

Inspector Carrigan snorted again, and I sensed that he was indeed thinking. "All right," he said, "if you can guarantee me that you'll keep a watch on him, I'll release the little devil. I'll have the papers ready tomorrow morning. But in return, I expect to get reports of his every move, or else it's your pretty head in the noose."

"I understand," I said, "and I will do anything to see that Harry gets what he deserves."

Taking my leave of Scotland Yard, I returned home to Queen Anne street, wearied from the strange and trying day, but knowing that there was little time to waste. Having achieved my objective of getting Harry released from that horrible cell, I now had to figure out how free him from constant police scrutiny. By the time the evening clock chimed ten, my plan was formulated. It was audacious, almost laughable, and perhaps it was simply the lateness of the hour, but I was convinced it would work.

I spent most of the next morning setting the plan in action, then travelled once more to Scotland Yard, in order to retrieve Harry. As the two of us were being marched out of the premises by Inspector Carrigan and a covey of constables, I managed to whisper to Harry the basics of my plan. Our procession went without incident until we were outside the massive iron gate, at which point Harry shouted: "You traitor!" and with a powerful shove, pushed me down onto the pavement. Police whistles pierced the air as a circle of constables stood round me, trying to help. I watched as Harry darted in and out of the crowds on the Embankment eluding the police. A few moments later, a breathless PC reappeared to inform the inspector, "He's gone, sir, he jumped into a cab and it sped away."

"Well, try to find it!" Inspector Carrigan roared, and a dozen constables rushed away. Then he turned on me. "Look what you have caused, madam!"

"I am sorry," I panted, "but I fear I am also hurt. Please help me up."

As the remaining constables helped me to my feet, I heard

a familiar voice call out: "Heavens, child, is that you?" and saw a small, white-haired woman rushed towards me. "Dear, dear, are you all right?" she clucked.

"Now who's this?" Inspector Carrigan demanded.

"Martha Hudson," the woman answered, "a family friend, you might say. How fortunate 'tis that I happened to be passing this way. Are you hurt, love?"

"I am not sure," I answered honestly.

"Come home with me, dear, I'll make you some tea," Mrs. Hudson said. I looked to the inspector who grumbled, "Fine, fine, get out of here."

We hailed a cab and Mrs. Hudson helped me into it. As we sped off to Baker street, she said: "I hope that wasn't too hard of a shove, ducks."

"It had to be convincing, Harry," I said, as he pulled off the grey wig and started to unbutton the black dress that had transformed him into a reasonable likeness of John's former landlady! I prayed the rest of the charade was as convincing.

The real Mrs. Hudson greeted us at the door of 221b, and I once more thanked her profusely for the loan of the clothes, which had been placed inside the cab that I had retained for the sole purpose of spiriting Harry away and facilitating his quick change. Mrs. Hudson had accepted this bizarre affair with a sense of amusement (I imagine that, over the years, she must have gotten accustomed to all manner of strangeness) and further displayed her angelic nature by agreeing to put up Harry in the now-empty rooms that had once housed Sherlock Holmes until this business was concluded.

It seemed clear that the only way to exonerate Harry was to find the missing boys ourselves. I was convinced that Harry had indeed seen the kidnapper's fleeing coach, but refused to believe it had simply disappeared into thin air. "Tell me everything again, Harry," I said, pacing the floor of the empty (and now somehow soulless) apartment, and he repeated his story, but it still made no sense. After a day of searching for answers, we retired, exhausted. Leaving Harry to the able care of Mrs. Hudson, I returned home.

I was awakened from a late sleep the next morning by Missy, who informed me that another letter from John had arrived. Without rising from the bed (my hip was still sore from yesterday's adventure), I tore open the envelope and read:

> *Dearest;*
> *I must report a singular occurrence that took place at last night's lecture. While looking out at the audience, I was suddenly struck by the ap-*

pearance of an elderly gentleman who was regarding me with great intensity. My initial reaction was to shout: "Holmes!" for so I thought it was, in one of his disguises. Seeing the man so distracted me that I momentarily lost track of my speech, and by the time I looked up from my notes, he was gone. Had it really been he? Or am I just so involved with the man and his exploits that I am seeing apparitions of him? I had no way of discovering the truth, as the very floor of the lecture hall seemed to open up and swallow the man in front of me, so fast was his disappearance. Perhaps, darling, I am working too hard.

I finished the letter and set it next to its cherished brethren on the table beside the bed, and went about my morning routine. It was while I was dressing that the words from John's letter struck me, and suddenly Harry's story did not seem so ridiculous.

I set out for Baker Street at once, stopping on the way at a stationers to buy a street map, which I carried into the empty rooms and unfolded on the floor before Harry. "Show me where you were when you saw the coach," I asked.

He pointed to a spot on the South Bank near the Tower Bridge. "Right around here, near Pickle Herring street."

"Yet the children were abducted from Mayfair, all the way over here. Why take them all the way across the river to that place in particular?"

"Maybe he fancies himself a bit of old Dickie the Third, you know, locking up the young princes in the Tower o' London?"

"No, there's another reason, and to prove it we must find that building that opened up and swallowed the carriage."

Despite the grim, grey sky, the streets remained dry as we travelled by cab virtually the entire length of the city and across the London Bridge, before finally disembarking on Tooley Street near London Bridge Station. "This way," Harry said, leading me down an alleyway, at the end of which stood a large, drab building. "There it is," he called, and we rushed towards it, only to find that the large barn-style doors were held fast by a padlock. Obviously, the mysterious tenant was out, having locked the door behind him.

"We need to get inside here," I said, examining the front of the building.

"Well, ducks, I figure either we can break that window over there and climb through, risking life and limb, or you can give me a hairpin," Harry answered.

Michael Mallory

"A hairpin? Are you serious?"

He grinned back at me. "'Course I am. Didn't I ever tell you my dear ol' Da was a locksmith?"

I handed him the pin, and true to his word, the lock was open and on the ground within a minute. The building was dark, but not so dark that we could not make out a strange cage-like box that occupied most of the space inside. "That wasn't there when I peeped through the shutters," Harry said, fingering one of the steel walls. "What is it?"

"Unless I have become completely addled, it is a lift, probably designed to raise and lower building materials. It is certainly big enough to hold a two-wheeler coach and horse, and the reason you did not see it before is because it was descending when you looked in."

"But who in blazes would want to go under the ground... *Gor*!" Harry said, slapping his forehead with his palm. "Half o' blinkin' London, that's who."

"Yes, Harry, the same realization came to me this morning, but I had to make sure I was right. This must be the lowering mechanism," I said, touching a loop of rope that ran through a pulley on the ceiling and then disappeared through a hole cut into the floor of the lift. We both took hold of the rope and pulled, though the platform dropped so easily that I could have managed it alone. We descended into what should have been darkness, but someone had thoughtfully placed oil lanterns in niches carved into the walls of the shaft at various intervals.

Before long we bumped to a stop, and in the dim light of the lanterns I could see a wide passageway containing an open bale of hay (as well as other, less pleasant, traces of a horse's recent inhabitation) and lengths of huge iron pipes. Directly behind us was a more nostalgic sight: the wide spiral staircase that provided street access to this underground thoroughfare. We were in the Tower Subway, a pedestrian tunnel running under Thames that was closed upon the opening of the Tower Bridge, some ten years ago, and eventually forgotten. Although somebody had obviously remembered it.

"You think the tykes are in the subway?" Harry asked.

If they are not, I'll eat that hay bale," I said, as we stepped onto a wooden platform that had been erected over the water mains that the tunnel now housed. We had travelled only a few yards over the planking, past the first great arch of the tunnel, when I heard a young voice call out: "He's coming back!"

Following the voice, I ran to the next arch and was greeted by a sight that nearly shattered my heart. In the midst of a dirty, makeshift camp were the two boys, watching us with eyes rimmed with fear. A sob rose up in my throat upon seeing that the brute who had brought them down into this dank netherworld had also left them tied up in their chairs with ropes that visibly chafed their wrists and ankles.

"Please don't hurt us," the younger of the two said in a tiny, frightened voice.

"No, darling," I said, rushing to him and smothering his brow with kisses, insufficient compensation for his ordeal.

"Who are you?" the elder boy asked.

"We are friends who have come to get you out of here," I assured him. "When will your captor return?"

"Soon," the elder boy said. "He usually leaves this time of day, but he comes back quickly."

Harry had already begun to saw through the ropes with a pen knife. When he had released the younger boy, he said, "I'll bet you're the one who lost his little bear."

The boy's face instantly lit up. "You've found my Teddy?"

"Keeping it safe just for your return," Harry said, and taking the younger boy's hand, while I took the hand of his brother, we started back towards the lift. A voice from the shadows, however, stopped us.

"Well, well, well," Inspector Carrigan said, raising his revolver, "both the conspirators and their prey are found in the warren."

"I'm glad to see you, Inspector," I said. "We have found the boys."

"And I have found you. Come over here lads." Reluctantly, the boys joined him on his side of the revolver, which unfortunately was still trained on Harry and I. "Recovering the missing children and capturing the kidnappers, not a bad day's work," he gloated.

The older of the two boys cried: "They are not — " but the inspector cut him off, saying: "Shush now, lads, I have the situation in hand." Then turning to me, he sneered: "You really must have thought I was just another ruddy stupid copper, like the ones in those worthless detective stories people write. But I didn't believe you for a second, madam. I had a tail on you from the moment you left the yard, and I knew, sooner or later, you and your friend here would lead us to the boys. So why don't we all go topside, real quiet like. And don't even think about trying to escape again, because I've got men surrounding this building."

Inspector Carrigan then motioned us onto the lift with his revolver and instructed Harry and I to operate the pulley, which was considerably more difficult for the journey upwards, particularly in light of the three extra bodies on board (and I could only wonder at the level of strength required to raise the platform with a horse and coach!). By the halfway point my strength was spent and it was up to Harry to bring us to the surface. But even before we arrived, we could hear the sounds of chaos taking place just above our heads. As we broke through into daylight, we were greeted by the sight of two PC's struggling mightily with a large, burly man dressed in the garb of a cabman, just outside the doors of the shed.

One of the constables addressed Inspector Carrigan. "We found this man snooping around the building, sir. He took one look at us and tried to run, but we got him. He's a strong one, though!"

"That's him!" cried the younger boy, "that's the one who took us!"

"What? What's that?" the inspector muttered, trying to follow the line of confusion.

At that very moment another man appeared, and only the unexpected presence of my husband would have been a more welcome sight. "All right, Carrigan, you have me here," Sir Melville Macnaghten bristled, "now what is it that is so beastly important?" While I could not claim to know Sir Melville well, he was an ally of John's and I had been a guest at the dinner party celebrating his ascension to the head of the Criminal Investigation Division.

"I wanted you to be here when I solved the Radford case, sir," the inspector said, and pointing at us, added: "These two are the kidnappers."

Sir Melville glanced at me and then did a "take" that would have done Harry proud. "Mrs. Watson, is it not?" he said, "What are you doing here?"

"It will take a long time to explain, Sir Melville," I said, "but you have no idea how happy I am to see you."

The inspector eyed us warily. "You know each other?"

"Of course we do," Sir Melville replied, "her husband has helped out the Yard on many occasions. A kidnapper, you say? You must be daft, man!" Then a smile softened his face. "Ah, but these must be the missing boys. Glad to have you back, lads." He then turned to the still struggling cabman. "Who is this?"

"I... don't know, sir," Inspector Carrigan said sickly. "My men caught him sneaking around."

"Me name's Hoskins, an' I drive a hack, that's all," the man declared.

"He is the blackguard who took us away!" the older boy cried, and Hoskins countered the boy's defiance with a murderous look. Meanwhile, the younger one dashed in front of Harry and I, as though to protect us, and cried: "And this man and this lady are the ones who found us, they are not criminals!"

"I see," Sir Melville said. "So Mrs. Watson and her friend discovered the whereabouts of the missing boys, while the foot constables managed to capture the kidnapper. Tell me, Carrigan, what, exactly, was your participation in this effort?"

The inspector's mouth worked up and down, though no sound came out. He was still attempting to speak as Sir Melville instructed a half-dozen of his officers to take the villainous Hoskins to the Yard. Then kneeling down to face the boys, Sir Melville said, "I wish half of my men were as brave as you lads. But now we must get you home to your parents."

As the two boys ran to the police carriage, Inspector Carrigan finally found his voice. "Sir, I would like to say — "

"You may say whatever you like this afternoon in my office, Carrigan," Sir Melville snapped. "Now then, Mrs. Watson and Mr..."

"Benbow, sir," Harry said.

"Mr. Benbow. May I offer you the comfort of my carriage back to Scotland Yard. I am afraid we still must trouble you for your statements." Our last view of Inspector Carrigan as we drove away was of him throwing his bowler hat to the ground and stomping it as though it were a snake.

In the carriage, Harry asked: "How do you figure this Hoskins bloke even knew about the lift in the subway?"

"I am sure we will learn upon questioning him," Sir Melville said, "though I could not help but notice the man's hands. They were quite scarred and several of his fingernails were discoloured and misshapen, not the sort of marks one normally sees on the hands of a hackney driver. They are more indicative of a labourer, particularly one who works with heavy tools. A sandhog, for instance, or perhaps a pipe fitter."

"Are you saying that he might have worked on the crew that installed the water pipes in the subway?" I asked.

"It is a theory, nothing more," Sir Melville responded.

"*Gor*," said Harry, "if I didn't know better, I'd swear I was in the presence o' Sherlock Holmes himself!"

The smile of satisfaction was still on Sir Melville's face when we reached Scotland Yard.

THE ADVENTURE OF
THE NEFARIOUS NEPHEW

Although he was quite slender, Sir Peter Swindon managed to puff out his chest like a pigeon while strutting like a popinjay, his white periwig standing in for a bird's natural crest. I have no doubt that this posturing was impressing some within the courtroom, though I felt it bordered on the comical.

"Now then, Dr. Watson," he said, absently brushing his moustache with the edge of his monocle, "you were engaged by Scotland Yard to examine the body of Humphrey Jafford, were you not?"

"I was," my husband answered from the witness stand.

"And what did your examination reveal?"

From one coat pocket John withdrew a small notebook, and from the other, a pair of spectacles that he had only recently been required to obtain. Using the detailed and terminology of the medical profession, he went on to describe the gruesome fact that Mr. Jafford had died as the result of a severe blow to the head from a heavy object. "Judging from the position of the body and the direction of the blood flow from the wound," he added, "it seems clear that Mr. Jafford was facing his attacker, and fell backwards upon receiving the blow."

"Facing his attacker," Sir Peter mused. "And why should he not face his attacker, since he knew him so well." This statement was pointedly directed towards the defendant, Owen Jafford, the victim's nephew. Strikingly handsome, if somewhat dandified, Owen Jafford was marked by one curious fluke of nature: despite his youth, his hair, which was worn on the longish side, was almost totally white.

But if the prosecutor's objective was to rattle the defendant with his accusation he failed, as young Jafford merely looked away in bored fashion.

"Is it possible, Dr. Watson," Sir Peter went on, "that a heavy, silver-headed walking stick, much like the one the defendant carries, could have been the object that was used to kill Humphrey Jafford?"

"It is possible, yes."

"I see. Was there anything else that you observed while examining the deceased?"

"Yes. The placement of the wound, on the right side of the head, indicated that his assailant was a left-handed man." I looked back at the now-frowning defendant and noticed that he was indeed holding his walking stick with his left hand. "And then there was the matter of his closed fist," John offered.

"Pray, explain yourself, doctor," Sir Peter said.

"The late Mr. Jafford's left hand was tightly clenched, a muscle contraction that does not occur naturally in death. It occurred to me that he might have been grasping something in his hand at the time of his death, so I asked Inspector Laurie to pry the man's hand open."

"And what did the inspector find?"

"Hairs," John said. "White hairs."

Sir Peter turned to glare once more at Owen Jafford. "White hairs found in the hand of a man who had been killed by a left-handed assailant; the evidence speaks clearly for itself, m'lud," he announced. "I put it to the court that, having been informed of his dying uncle's intentions to disinherit him, Owen Jafford took it upon himself to speed along his uncle's appointment with the angels before any new will could be drawn up. The two argued, may even have struggled, ergo the hairs in Humphrey Jafford's clenched hand. The encounter rushed to a deadly conclusion when Owen Jafford raised his stick — " and here the prosecutor thrust his hand dramatically in the air — "and struck!"

The spectators in the court chamber collectively gasped at the theatrics.

"Thank you, Dr. Watson," Sir Peter concluded and returned to his table.

It was now time for Mr. Strang, the counsel for the defence, to strike back at John's damaging testimony, which, I feared, was in for a severe raking. I was therefore quite surprised when the opposing barrister calmly announced: "May it please the court, m'lud, I have no questions for Dr. Watson."

"Indeed, Mr. Strang?" remarked the grim-faced Judge Wilkins, who seemed quite surprised himself. "Very well, Dr. Watson, you may step down."

John did so, striding to the back of the courtroom to take

a seat beside me. I squeezed his hand in support of a job well done. While I knew John had offered expert testimony in many cases in the past, I had never before seen him in this environment. In fact, this was my first experience with the criminal court system of Great Britain. I would not have been here at all were it not for my desire to be near John at all times during this break in his successful lecture tour.

Mr. Strang then announced: "I would like to summon to the stand Lady Emmaline Belgrave," and the confused reaction of Sir Peter indicated that he knew nothing of this surprise witness.

A small, elegant woman of middle years, clad in a fine crushed velvet dress the colour of berries, made her way to the stand. Mr. Strang bumbled along behind her, revealing a natural Pickwickian sort of dignity that stood in contrast to the affected theatrical pomposity of his opponent.

"Now then, Lady Emmaline," he began, "you have heard it stated that Humphrey Jafford met his untimely death on the evening of January the twelfth, 1904, sometime between eight o'clock, when his servant delivered a brandy to him in his library, and half-past eleven, when the same servant checked upon him."

"Oh, yes, indeed," she chirped.

"And at that time, Lady Emmaline, where were you?"

"I was at the Royal Opera House in Covent Garden."

"Were you alone?"

"Quite."

"While you were there, did you see anyone who is perhaps in this courtroom?"

"Oh, yes," she said, smiling, "I saw that young gentleman over there, Mr. Jafford."

A loud rumble of murmurs now broke out within the courtroom, prompting the judge to call for order. When it had been restored, Mr. Strang continued.

"How long were you at the opera, Lady Emmaline?" he asked.

"Curtain rings up exactly at eight, so I must have been there from about half-past seven," she replied. "I like to sit in my box and watch the comings and goings of the other patrons. Since it was Wagner night, the curtain did not ring down until nearly midnight."

"And Owen Jafford was there the entire time?"

"Oh, yes, the entire time."

"So there is no way he could have been in Earl's Court on that evening, murdering his uncle."

The witness shuddered. "How dreadful, even to contemplate."

"Thank you, Lady Emmaline," the portly barrister said, returning to his seat. John, meanwhile, leaned over to me and whispered into my ear: "There's a development for you!"

It was abundantly clear, however, that Sir Peter was not about to take this development peacefully. He virtually leapt to his feet and approached the stand. "Lady Emmaline, prior to the evening when you say you saw the defendant at the opera, had you ever met him before?"

"Oh, no," she replied.

"Indeed? How was it, then, that you came to notice, and keep under surveillance for nearly four hours, a man of whom you had no prior knowledge?"

"As I said, I like to watch people from my box. It so happens that I have been looking for a walking stick to get as a gift for my husband, Lord Belgrave. When I noticed Mr. Jafford take his seat, I said to myself: 'That young man is carrying the exact walking stick I have been seeking.' I made it a point to seek him out after the opera to ask him from whence he had obtained it. I fear the other patrons must have thought me the victim of a robbery, for I ran after him calling, 'Young man, please stop!'"

A titter of gentle laughter ruffled the crowd at this. Sir Peter, however, seemed not amused. "M'lud," he said, "in light of this unexpected testimony, I beg the court time to reevaluate our case." I noticed a smugly satisfied smile on the face of Mr. Strang.

"Very well," Judge Wilkins ruled, "we shall reconvene at ten o'clock tomorrow." As Sir Peter walk back to his chair, I noticed that he faltered slightly, and for a moment I thought it might be more theatrics, but the concerned expression on John's face convinced me otherwise. Within seconds we were at his side.

"Has the pain returned?" John asked.

"Only slightly," Sir Peter responded, though his ashen face told a more serious tale.

"I insist on giving you a thorough examination," my husband said. "Chest pains are not to be ignored."

"Accompany me to my office, then, for I have no time to follow you to yours."

Even though the walk from the Old Bailey to the Inner Temple was an easy one, John decided that a coach ride would be best for the ailing barrister. Once within the Temple, I waited in a clerk-filled antechamber while John conducted his examination in Sir Peter's private office, after which I was allowed inside.

"I have warned you, Sir Peter, against the continued strain of two many cases in succession," my husband was saying. "After this one it is imperative that you rest."

"After I forfeit this one, you mean," he said gloomily, all traces of the former popinjay having disappeared.

"The defendant does appear to have a strong alibi," I stated.

"That woman was lying, Mrs. Watson," he replied, "The evidence against Jafford is simply too strong, as Strang must have realized, which is why he has miraculously produced an eyewitness at the eleventh hour to put him in a different place altogether."

"Please, Sir Peter, you must not excite yourself," John cautioned.

"But can't you see that the young scoundrel is going to get away with it?" the barrister cried. "I have until tomorrow morning to try and break this alibi, or the case is lost."

"Perhaps you could beat Lady Emmaline's statements down on the stand," John suggested.

"No, no, no, you saw how she charmed everyone in the courtroom. I would come off as a reprehensible bully. The question we should be asking is, why would a woman of her station be lying for a young rotter. She must know him, somehow. If only I could prove that, it would destroy her story. But how could I be expected to do it by ten o'clock tomorrow?"

"Well, it will do absolutely no good to work yourself into a froth," John said. "I am going to prescribe a sedative for you so that you will at least get a decent night's rest."

"Dr. Watson, if you could guarantee that you would have the solution to my problem by the time I awaken tomorrow morning, I would gladly ingest anything," Sir Peter said. "If not, I must continue to work, through the night if necessary."

"I accept the challenge," I blurted out, prompting John to turn and stare at me, open-mouthed. "Before the clock strikes ten tomorrow, you shall have an answer."

"But how could you...ah, I see," the barrister said, his eyes darting back and forth between John and me. "You shall get Sherlock Holmes to work on the problem, eh?"

"If he is available. Right, darling?" I said, watching John's face begin to redden.

"Fair enough," Sir Peter said, suddenly relaxing. "Go ahead, Dr. Watson, do your worst."

John stepped out to talk to one of the law clerks, sending him to the nearest chemist for a powder. After instructing Sir Peter as to its administration, he escorted him to the street and hailed a coach to carry him to his home. Then, and only then, did John speak to me.

"What in heaven's name did you mean by promising to solve his case for him?" he demanded. "And what is this business of getting Holmes involved! You know perfectly well he is off somewhere on this American crusade of his and cannot even be contacted!"

"John, I did not promise that Mr. Holmes would be involved," I said. "I suggested that he may help if he were available, which, as we know, he is not. Nor did I say that we would solve Sir Peter's case. What I said was that we would have an answer for him. The answer might well be, 'Sorry, we cannot help you.'"

John was glaring at me now, and doing a rather good impersonation of a smoldering log in a fireplace. "Oh, don't look at me that way, dear," I protested. "You saw the state the poor man was in. This was the only way he would have agreed to your prescription."

John sighed. "Yes, you may be right. Still, I don't like to see him get his hopes up only to be dashed."

"Then we must do whatever we can to see that his hopes are not dashed," I replied.

Since John had to return to his surgery that afternoon (rather than atrophy as a result of his recent absence, his practice had seemed to grow), he headed off in one direction and I another. I arrived home, chilled from the brisk January weather, to find Missy, our maid, dusting the bookshelf. "Thank you, dear, for cleaning this off for me," I said, pulling down the Debrett's that we had somehow acquired, yet rarely used.

I quickly found the entry for Lord Hugh Belgrave, but discovered it to be less than revealing, being largely concerned with his lineage. It did, however, confirm that his lordship had taken a wife named Emmaline, a union which produced a son named Richard. I read the entry over and over, looking for some kind of clue, which, of course, was not there. Then, as Missy continued her chores, I sat back and tried to imagine what Sherlock Holmes would do in this situation, given the scanty facts. The answer came quickly.

I snatched up yesterday's edition of the *Times* and turned to the theatre listings. A cry of delight escaped my lips (which rather startled poor Missy) as I read the schedule for the Royal Opera House.

When John arrived home several hours later, he was surprised to find me in evening wear. "Where are we going?" he asked.

"To the opera, John," I replied. "It's Wagner night."

A light, but not altogether unpleasant, snow salted our clothing us as we stood in a queue at the box office of the opera house. Our seats were not particularly good, though to be honest, I have never been much of an enthusiast for Wagner, favouring less portentous music. But witnessing the performance was only a secondary reason for my presence. After searching virtually the entire house bottom-to-top, I finally spotted Lady Emmaline, in an upper loge box, seated next to a young man. I kept my attention focused on her throughout most of the first act, and at the first interval, watched as she and her companion exited through the back. Quickly rising from my seat, I started to slide past John.

"Where are you going in such a hurry?" he asked.

"I must not lose Lady Emmaline," I responded.

"I am coming with you," he said, rising himself.

"No, she might recognize you from the trial. I must do this alone." Leaving him, I made my way up the aisle and entered the crowded foyer, where the chances of finding one person in particular seemed impossible. Being rather tall, however, I was able to peer over the heads of most of the multitude. Before long I spotted Lady Emmaline Belgrave standing at the bar next to her young companion, who was sipping a brandy. As I fought my way through the throng to get to them, I realized I had but one quick chance to try and obtain the information I was seeking. I also realized that now was not the time for subtleties. "Lady Emmaline, isn't it?" I called, as soon as I was within earshot, and the woman turned to me.

"Yes?"

"I thought so," I said, wedging myself next to her. "Perhaps you don't remember me, but we met through a mutual friend, Owen Jafford."

But before she could reply, her young companion spun around and faced me. "Do we know you, madam?" he demanded.

"Dickie," she scolded, "don't be so dreadfully rude."

"I am sorry," I went on, "I was just telling Lady Emmaline that we have a mutual friend, Owen Jafford — "

Dickie Belgrave's darkly handsome face melted into a black scowl. "Never heard of the blighter," he said sharply, "and I will thank you, madam, to mind your own business. Come along mother, let's go back." She was still protesting as the young brute pulled her through the crowd towards the stairs.

It was obvious to me that the name Owen Jafford meant something to Dickie Belgrave, something he chose not to acknowledge.

I quickly returned to John, who was chatting amiably with another patron. "Darling, let's go," I said, excitedly.

"But we have only seen one act," he replied.

"Please, John," I entreated.

"Oh, very well." Excusing himself from his previous conversation, he accompanied me to the coat room.

In the freezing cab on the way home, I told him of my encounter with Lady Emmaline though, to my surprise, he failed to share my excitement. "That was a rather foolhardy thing to do, Amelia," he uttered. "You tipped them off to your game."

"There was no time to do anything else," I protested. "But if Sir Peter put Dickie Belgrave on the stand — "

"Belgrave would deny knowing Jafford, just like as he denied it to you," John said. "And being the son of a peer, he would be believed." Then taking my icicle hand in his, he added gently: "I am sorry, Amelia, but the law requires proof, not merely intuition. It may be true that Lady Emmaline and her son are both lying, but how can you prove it? Ah, here we are." The cab pulled to a stop in front of our home.

Spending the time required to prepare for bed in silent rumination, I had to accept the fact that he was right. We had failed. More precisely, *I* had failed, and Owen Jafford was soon to be a free man.

"Aren't you coming to bed?" John asked.

"I think I will stay up for a bit and read," I said. "Maybe it will drive away this horrid sense of frustration." From the shelf I selected Mr. Dickens' *Christmas Books*, which I had been meaning to reread since the yuletide, and turned to my favourite among these tales, *A Christmas Carol*. I savoured the familiar prose until my eyes began to tire and droop, and with growing effort I read the description of the second midnight spirit:

> *It's hair, which hung about its neck and down its back, was white as if with age; and yet the face had not a wrinkle on it, and the tenderest bloom was on the skin.*

Whether I had actually dropped off into sleep or not, I do not know. All I can recall is suddenly sitting up, vividly awake, a light beam having been switched on in my mind. I had found the flaw in Lady Emmaline Belgrave's testimony!

Being of generous nature, I let John sleep rather than rushing into the bedroom and waking him up with the news, though I myself tossed and turned excitedly throughout the night. Early the next morning, however, we were en route to the home of Sir Peter Swindon to tell him of my realization. His initial reaction was all that I had hoped for.

"That is brilliant, Mrs. Watson!" he cried, but then ruined it by adding: "If only you were a man, you would make a splendid lawyer." Why, oh why is it that so many men would just as soon accept the existence of Mr. Wells' Martian invaders than believe that a woman is born with a brain? I opened my mouth to respond to him, but before I could, he let out a gasp and clutched his chest, then slowly sank down to one knee.

"Sir Peter!" John cried, rushing to him and helping him off the floor to a nearby couch.

"This is the worst one yet," gasped the lawyer.

"We must get you to the hospital immediately," John declared.

"But the case. . ." Sir Peter croaked.

"The case is not worth risking your life over," John replied, sternly. The judge will simply have to delay the proceedings until you are well."

A sardonic smile rose through the fear and pain on the lawyer's face. "Strang would not let that go unchallenged," he uttered. "He is holding all the cards at present, and would protest that this was nothing more than a confusion tactic. He would badger Wilkins for a dismissal, and likely get it."

As I watched and listened helplessly, an idea began to form in my mind, one that was so audacious, so riotous, that I tried to push it out, but it would not go. "Perhaps I can help," I offered. "What if I were to question Lady Emmaline in court?"

"You?"

"Yes, along with a few visual aids such as. . . well, might I borrow a suit of yours, Sir Peter?"

"A suit?" he queried. "You mean you wish to appear before the Bench posing as me?"

I wanted to tell him that I was simply attempting to meet his own criteria for legal acceptability — namely, being of the male sex — but I fought the urge down. Instead I said: "I know it probably sounds insane — "

"Because it is insane," John interjected. "You must forgive my wife, Sir Peter. She was an actress in her youth and sometimes forgets that all the world is not a stage."

I was about to rebuff John's comment when I noticed that Sir Peter was regarding me with renewed interest. Through the pain, I thought I detected a shining curiosity in his eyes. Playing up to this interest, I said: "This may be the only chance to bring Mr. Jafford to justice."

"Do you think you could do it?" he asked.

"No," John returned, "I positively forbid — "

"Yes," I answered firmly, ignoring my husband. "I watched you yesterday in court, observed your manner and stance. As we are roughly the same height, it would be a matter of removing my cosmetics, fixing my hair, fashioning a moustache and lowering my voice. And I have experience, of course — I once understudied the role of Portia."

"I know why you are doing this, Amelia," John said conspiratorially, "and I assure you, you do not have to prove anything to either of us."

"Whatever do you mean, darling?" I asked, innocently.

"Amelia, we are talking about the King's Bench!" John suddenly cried. "The Old Bailey is not a theatre!"

"Don't be too sure, old fellow," Sir Peter said, ending the argument.

I quickly dressed in an old tweed suit of Sir Peter's and set about duplicating his visage over my own. Letting down my hair, I flattened it as much as possible and hid the excess under the shirt collar. Soot from the chimney turned my auburn tresses black like Sir Peter's, and I carefully trimmed some ends, which I attached under my nose with paste to create a moustache. In his closet I found an old, rather dusty, periwig and an unused monocle. Strutting like a popinjay, I made my entrance into the living room.

"God help us," John muttered. "The resemblance is better than I would have predicted, but still, you will never get away with it."

"People tend to see what they expect to see," Sir Peter said, adding: "It just might work."

It was that quietly-spoken encouragement that carried me all the way to the Old Bailey where, less than an hour later, properly robed and bewigged, I faced an audience consisting of judge, jury and on-lookers (including, I noticed, Dickie Belgrave). I silently prayed, then called Lady Emmaline Belgrave to the stand. Immediately, Judge Wilkins interrupted.

"Counsel for the prosecution does not sound like himself today," he said, frowning, and for a moment I fought down panic. I recovered well enough to say: "I fear I am catching cold, m'lud."

"I see," he acknowledged, albeit skeptically.

"Lady Emmaline," I began, "yesterday you testified that you had never before met, or even seen Owen Jafford prior to the opera."

"That is true," she confirmed.

"Where were you when you first noticed him?"

"In my regular box in the loge."

"And where was he?"

"Down below, on the orchestra level."

"Quite a distance," I noted, strutting and fiddling with the monocle, while trying to keep my face down. "And tell me again what you thought upon seeing Mr. Jafford?"

"I said to myself: 'That young man is carrying the exact walking stick I have been looking for.'"

"Ah, yes, and then you told us that you ran after him shouting, 'Young man, please stop.'"

"That is true."

I took a deep breath. "I confess, Lady Emmaline, that I do not understand that. Anyone truly seeing Owen Jafford for the first time, especially from the distance of a loge box or from behind, would be excused for assuming that he was an elderly man, since his hair is white. Yet, by your own testimony, you knew him to be a young man, and even used that term to call after him — or so you claim. There is only one way, Lady Emmaline, that you could have assumed that Mr. Jafford was a youth of less than thirty, and that is if you had already been acquainted with him."

A murmur went through the courtroom.

"Well, I. . . I. . . " she stammered.

"What is the truth, Lady Emmaline?" I demanded. "How long have you known Owen Jafford? Long enough to lie on his behalf?"

What followed was chaos. Mr. Strang jumped up and began shouting objections, while at the same time, Lady Emmaline turned to her son and called out, "What should I say, Dickie?"

Leaping to his feet, Owen Jafford shouted back: "Say nothing, you senile old cat!"

"How dare you speak that way to my mother, Jaffie!" Dickie shouted back, and within seconds, the august proceeding was a shambles. Through all the shouting, however, I was able to hear Lady Emmaline's excited testimony, which was directed towards the judge. "They told me it would cause no harm to pretend I saw Jaffie at the opera," she was saying. "They said it was the only way Jaffie would be able to get the money he owes my Dickie."

Judge Wilkins, meanwhile, was pounding his gavel to the breaking point in the attempt to bring about order. Once it had finally been restored, he announced: "The prisoner at the bar will be remanded into custody until such time as I have had the opportunity to confer with counsel for both sides. I wish to see the prosecutor immediately." With that he stepped down from the bench and motioned for me to follow.

With considerable trepidation, I followed him to a surprisingly austere chamber located behind the courtroom, which was furnished only with a desk, two chairs, an odd framed painting or two, and an array of filled bookcases. He began to remove his robes and wig, and bid me do the same. The game was over. Slowly, and trembling with fear, I removed the garments and pulled the pasty moustache from my lip.

The judge's gaze turned into a stare, then a gape. "Good God!" he said, "I knew you weren't Swindon, but I had no idea you were a woman! Who in blazes are you, and where the devil is the real Swindon?"

Hesitantly, I introduced myself and explained that Sir Peter had suddenly taken ill and was under the care of my husband, emphasizing that John was vehemently opposed to my impersonation. There was no sense in ruining my husband's reputation as well.

"The doctor is a sensible man," he said.

"I know that, my lord," I said, softly.

"On the other hand, without this decidedly brazen act of yours, we would never have got the goods on Jafford, would we?"

"You, too, believed him to be guilty?"

"As sin. And quite honestly, were I prosecuting this case, faced with these peculiar circumstances, I might have condoned such extreme measures myself in order to convict the blackguard."

"Is that why you did not expose me at once?"

He shook his head. "I did not expose you because I did not want to reduce the courtroom to a circus until I figured out what your game was. But then I became rather interested in your line of questioning." Having said that, his face became quite stern. "But I must caution you in strongest terms not to attempt this again. Given the circumstances, the high regard in which I hold your husband and, frankly, the results, I am willing to overlook this absurd charade. But I will not be so forgiving in the face of any future assaults on the integrity of the Bench. And one more thing: you are not to tell another living soul what you have done here today. Is that clear?"

"Perfectly, my lord, and thank you," I said, sighing with relief.

The reaction from the excitement in the courtroom was still at such a pitch in the hallways of the Old Bailey that I was able to wedge past an army of reporters and slip out of the building unnoticed. Equally anonymously, I boarded the omnibus that carried me home.

John would demand a complete explanation of course, as would Sir Peter, though aside from them, I anticipated no difficulty in complying with Judge Wilkins command for silence. For even if I were to tell anyone of my escapade in court, who would believe it?

THE ADVENTURE OF THE JAPANESE SWORD

"What do you say we take a walking tour of San Francisco," my husband entreated. "We should experience the city. I understand there is an eating house here that actually serves buffalo meat."

"You can't be serious, darling," I moaned, falling back on the bed. After an entire week spent aboard ship followed by six more torturous days covering the American continent by train, I was in no condition to go traipsing through a strange city, particularly one that requires the traipser to be half mountain goat. And having seen a buffalo from the window of our train, I did not even want to contemplate dining on one. "Can't we stay in this evening, John, just the two of us?"

"But this is such a grand city, Amelia," he continued, displaying the unnaturally youthful cast that comes over him when he is truly excited, "I do not wish to waste a minute in seeing it again."

"Again?" I asked, raising my head from the pillow. "You have been here before?"

"Oh yes, years ago, before my army service. Haven't I told you that?"

"I think not. You know, dear, sometimes I worry that you deliberately hide details of your early life from me."

"Nonsense. You are not coming then?"

"Please, John, I must rest," I begged. "Perhaps by tomorrow I will be better able to conquer the colonies."

John left the hotel shortly thereafter to drink in the city before going to inspect the lecture hall where Friday evening he would be regaling the American multitude with his adventures in the company of Mr. Sherlock Holmes. (And how deliciously ironic that I had foresworn an early career on the stage only to marry a man who would embrace one in his middle years.) No sooner had he gone than I fell into a deep sleep, from which I was rudely awakened a mere hour-and-a-quarter later by a pounding at the door. Rising with effort, I discovered the caller was a young hotel bellboy brandishing a brown envelope. "Letter for you, ma'am," he said, thrusting the envelope in my hand. "I also have a message from a Dr. Watson."

"Oh?" I yawned, "what is it?"

"He put a call through to the desk downstairs and said to tell you that the sponsors of his speaking tour have arranged a dinner with a representative of the Mayor's office. He asks that you join him at eight o'clock at Dominico's restaurant in New Montgomery street."

After acknowledging the message, I waved the lad away and shut the door. I still did not feel like emerging from the comfortable hotel room, but if John thought it was important enough to send for me, I suppose I should at least try to make the effort to go. I then turned my attention to the envelope which was addressed to my husband, though I did not think he would mind if I opened it.

Instead of a letter, it contained a photograph of a woman wearing a bridal gown seated next to a man in formal wear, obviously a bride and groom. I stared at it uncomprehendingly at first, but then the image registered in my brain with searing clarity. The man in the picture was very young but his face was unmistakable. I was looking at an old wedding photograph *and my husband was the groom*! I had seen a photograph of Mary, John's late first wife — or at least the woman I had been told was his first wife — and this creature was not her. Was I indeed the *third* Mrs. John Watson?

As I groped for understanding, I flipped the photograph over and found on the back a handwritten note:

> *My dear Johnny,*
> *How long it has been! I read of your impending return to the city and decided that I must see you again. You will find me at the Hurley hotel in Post street.*
> *Yours, Caroline Adams*

Johnny? I read the note over and over and over again, feeling increasingly numb. How could he have kept a secret such as this from me? Now shockingly awake, I was determined to find out. I could hardly confront my husband in a restaurant, surrounded by the benefactors or our visit here, so quickly working to make myself a speck more presentable, I placed the photograph in my handbag and set out to call on this Caroline Adams.

Michael Mallory

As it turned out, the Hurley hotel was but a few blocks away, a trek that in London would have taken less than a quarter-hour. But in an unfamiliar city, shivering from the damp coldness that was, if anything, worse than London's, and unnerved by the clanging parade of cable-drawn railroad cars that held dominion over the streets, the journey seemed endless. It was with relief that I finally spotted a brass plaque that announced the garishly painted wooden edifice behind it as the Hurley Hotel. I marched in and inquired at the desk (which was manned by a fellow of lackadaisical demeanor) after Miss Adams, and was given a room number on the third floor, which I promptly located.

Bracing myself for whatever unpleasantness might follow, I rapped on the door of room 3-C, but received no answer. I rapped again, this time calling out Miss Adams' name, and was once more greeted with silence, though the door itself budged open. I stepped inside to find a room that was comfortably furnished, though the solitary wall lamp strained to provide enough illumination. "Miss Adams?" I called again, but no answer came. Assuming that she had stepped down the hall and would return momentarily, I opted to wait.

A closer examination of the room revealed a bookshelf filled to capacity with volumes that turned out to be elementary readers and school spelling books. Resting on top of the bookshelf was a large sheet of yellow paper on which was printed:

LET YOUR VOICE BE HEARD!
Fight the Union Labor Party and its insidious attempts to rid our fair city of an entire race of noble people who have caused no harm to anyone!

The hand bill went on to describe the plight of the Japanese community in San Francisco (which apparently was considerable) and how this Union Labor Party was advocating its complete separation, if not total exclusion, from the city. It was signed *Caroline F. Adams, Educator.*

I finished reading the document, which was written with fervour and passion, and then noticed a closed door, which I took to be entrance to the bedroom. Perhaps she was not down the hall, but sleeping. I knocked lightly and called her name, and when I received no response, I opened the door.

Oh, how I wish I had not.

The horrible sight on the bed made me cry out. Caroline Adams (for it surely was her) was laid out on the mattress as though posed, and her simple dress was stained by a dark red pool over

140

the stomach. Next to the body was very long, slender, slightly curved sword with writing characters that I guessed to be Japanese embossed on the handle. I did not need to approach Miss Adams closely to know that she was dead.

I found myself backing, almost involuntarily, away from the scene, out of the room and into the hallway, stopping only when I made contact with another body, one that put its hands on my shoulders!

"Whatsamatter with you?" a rough voice asked and I spun around, finding myself face to face with a coarse-featured man who reeked of alcohol.

"A woman is dead in there," I said, pointing to the room from which I had just emerged. "We must notify the police."

"I'm the hotel detective," the man replied, "I'll take care of it." He lurched past me and entered the room, emerging a few moments later, looking grim. "Yellow devils," he uttered.

"I beg your pardon, Mr...?"

"Hanrahan," he drawled, "and what I mean is the Japs. They're starting to form criminal gangs just like the Tongs, damn 'em. The Tongs, at least, have the decency to just kill each other and leave the real people alone, but this . . ." He regarded me with red, watery eyes. "What's your connection with this, anyway?"

"I came to call on Miss Adams and found her thus," I replied. "Why are you so sure it was the work of a Japanese killer?"

"Because I'm not stupid," he cried. "The murder weapon was left right there to tell us who was responsible. The devils want us to know who did it."

"But why would the very people she was trying to help kill her?"

"Trying to help?" he slurred, looking confused. "Look, lady, you're talkin' to a former Pinkerton's man, all right? I've got this under control, so why don't you just go back to Boston, or wherever that accent comes from, and stay out of my way. Go on, scram."

It is rare that I am at a loss for words, but the sheer ignorance and rudeness of this man succeeded in robbing me of coherent speech. I spun on my heel and marched back down the stairs to the lobby and out into the cool night. I continued to walk, propelled onward more out of anger than a desire to reach a destination, and as a result became quite lost in no time at all. I began to notice, however, that a private carriage had slowed down to stay apace beside me. At first I ignored it, a task that became more difficult when a white-whiskered face appeared out of the cab the window and called in a wheezy voice: "Would you care to join me inside, my dear?"

"I would not," I responded.

"I daresay I could make it worth your while," the man rejoined.

Irate at the implication, I turned and faced him directly. "And I daresay that I am not what you think I am!" I shouted.

"On the contrary, madam," came a low, familiar voice, "I know exactly who you are."

I gaped at the man, stunned. "Mr. — " was all I got out before he interrupted me, saying: "House, Sherrin House of Boulder, Colorado, at your service. Are you sure you won't join me?"

"Indeed, Mr...House, thank you," I said, stepping into the carriage and seating myself next to a white-haired and bewhiskered Sherlock Holmes!

"My compliments on the beard, Mr. Holmes," I replied, "Even this close I cannot detect a trace of spirit gum."

"Nor will you. The hair is all mine. The whiteness, of course, is fabricated. Where might I deliver this evening?"

I gave him the name of my hotel, which he relayed to the driver, and we set off. "What in Heaven's name are you doing in San Francisco?" I asked him.

"I swore that I would not rest until those responsible for Irene Adler's death have been brought to justice, and I have not. That quest has brought me here. But what of you, Mrs. Watson? I presume you are here with the good doctor, who I see is bringing his rampant storytelling skills to these shores, but that does not tell me what terrible trouble you have experienced this evening."

"How did you know that?"

"The angry tread of your step, the grim expression on your face, the unconscious opening and closing of your fist, really, madam, you might as well have been carrying a sign that read: *I am distraught.*"

"I have indeed had a dreadful evening," I said, telling him of my ghastly discovery in the Hurley hotel. He frowned slightly upon describing the nature of Miss Adams' fatal injury. "Something about this matter bothers you, Mr. Holmes?"

"The Japanese believe the belly to be the house of the soul," he stated. "You have heard of *hara kiri*, literally, belly-cutting? It is a form of ritual suicide and considered an honorable death. Murder, however, is not an honorable death, but a vengeful one. Given the placement of the wound, I doubt a real Japanese was involved at all. More likely someone attempting, quite clumsily, to make it appear that the murderer was Japanese. But you continue to withhold from me a vital fact regarding this deadly affair."

"I have told you everything, Mr. Holmes."

"Except what you were doing in the woman's hotel room in the first place."

I sighed. "Very well. I have reason to suspect that the dead woman was in reality John's first wife."

Surprise registered on the detective's lean, whiskered face. "Watson mentioned no such affair to me," he declared. "He was a bachelor up until the time he met Mary Morstan and remained completely devoted to her thereafter. And he was devastated when she and the child died."

"*Child?*" I cried. "What child?"

"Has he not told you? Mary was with child at the time of her death. It was a blow that nearly killed Watson. He was of no use to me for more than a year."

I leaned against the seat back, fighting tears, wondering how many more shatterings my heart would be able to withstand. I remained silent until the coach pulled up in front of the Westchester Hotel.

"This is your destination, I believe," Mr. Holmes gently prodded.

Clumsily, I stepped down from the cab.

"Mr. Watson, I beg you not to inform your husband of my presence here," he said. "It would only distract him while risking exposure for me. Our reunion will take place soon enough. I must now bid you good evening." With that, his vehicle sped away into the night.

I numbly made my way to our suite, only to find it a bee-hive of activity.

"Amelia!" John called as I appeared in the doorway, "where on earth have you been? I cancelled the dinner when I received word that you were feeling ill and came back here, but you were gone. Are you all right?"

"I do not know, John," I said, truthfully.

A uniformed policeman was hovering around the suite, along with a short, boyish-looking man whose face struggled to be seen from under a great shock of auburn hair. "Is there anything I can do, Dr. Watson?" he asked, and John introduced him to me as Mr. Bullock, an aide to the mayor of San Francisco, and our escort while in the city.

"There has been a terrible tragedy this evening, Amelia," John said. "A woman has been found murdered."

"How dreadful," I muttered. "Have you been called in on the case?"

Michael Mallory

"Not exactly, Mrs. Watson," Mr. Bullock answered. "Your husband's name and information regarding your visit here were found in a notebook in the woman's hotel room."

"An admirer?" I asked, hollowly.

"Someone I knew a long time ago," John answered, with a pained expression.

I was about to enquire further, when Mr. Bullock blurted out: "You know, Dr. Watson, calling you in on the case is not a bad idea. Perhaps you should go and inspect the murder scene yourself. After all, you are as experienced a detective as any on the force here."

"You flatter me," John said, puffing up slightly.

"I wish to go, too," I stated, "and please do not argue, John, since this is obviously the only way we shall be together this evening. Besides, I will be there to comfort you in your loss of an old acquaintance." Although he regarded me with a quizzical expression, John did not argue.

We journeyed by windy, noisy cable car to the Hurley hotel, where yet another police officer led us Caroline Adams room. "It would probably be best if you did not come inside the room until we get things cleaned up," Mr. Bullock told me. I was on the verge of protesting when I noticed that door to the room next to Miss Adams' creaking open. A woman with luxurious blonde hair peeked out and motioned me over. "What's going on over there?" she asked.

"It seems the woman who lived there has been murdered," I replied.

Her eyes widened. "Go on! C'mon in and tell me all about it," she said, opening the door and pulling me through. Introducing herself as Sally Probert, the woman pressed me for details of the slaying and reacted to each gossipy tidbit with a mixture of horror and excitement. For my part, I used this opportunity to find out more about Caroline Adams.

"She was a teacher, but not in the schools," Sally said. "She taught English to little Japanese kids, and sometimes to their folks. That was kind of a crusade of hers, but it wasn't very popular. A lot of people around here want to run the Asiatics out of town, not teach them to read."

"So I've gathered," I said. "That horrid Mr. Hanrahan seems eager to blame the murder on a Japanese criminal ring without even considering other possibilities. Almost too eager, in fact."

"Well, I think I would notice a Japanese gang wandering around," she replied. "But I haven't seen anybody unusual, except for that workman yesterday."

"Workman?"

"Yeah, some guy carrying a big long pipe on his shoulder. Big guy. I figured he was here to do a plumbing job or something, but it must've gotten cancelled, because the water was never shut off."

The voices from the room next door were getting louder and more animated, so after promising to keep her informed, I took my leave of Sally and stepped back into the hallway. As I approached the open door of 3-C I heard a voice shout: "And would you mind telling me how someone carrying a weapon the size of a Japanese sword could walk right past the hotel detective unseen?"

"They're tricky devils," slurred Hanrahan, more visibly intoxicated than when I had left him, who was rigorously being questioned by a plainclothes police sergeant. From the bedroom came two uniformed men carrying Caroline's body on a stretcher, and I quickly stepped inside the room to allow them to pass through the door, shuddering as they went by.

"At least tell me the name of the woman you say found the body," the sergeant demanded. "You did get her name, didn't you?"

At that exact moment, Hanrahan wobbled his head in my direction. "That's her right there in the hallway!" he bellowed, levelling a finger at me.

"My wife?" John shouted.

"The man is obviously mistaken," Mr. Bullock charged.

"What the man is, obviously, is stinking drunk," the sergeant said. "Get him out of here and find a charge to arrest him on." Another uniformed policeman took hold of Hanrahan and bodily drug him out of the room and down the hall, the detective's protests trailing behind him like so much smoke.

"I hope you realize, Sergeant Kellin, that Mayor Schmitz will accept nothing less than a full-scale effort dedicated to rounding up the yellow thugs that are responsible for this," Mr. Bullock declared.

"You may inform his honour that all effort will be made to find *the killer or killers*," the sergeant replied, pointedly.

Mr. Bullock's eyes narrowed. "It sounds as though you don't believe that the Asiatics are behind this."

"Motive, Bullock, what's the motive? Tell me that. And then tell me how somebody snuck a three-and-a-half-foot sword through a hotel lobby without anyone seeing it."

As this argument was taking place, I was inching over to the bookcase, prepared to "discover" the printed hand bill that I had noted earlier, but to my surprise I found that the paper was no

longer there. I glanced quickly around the room, but it was nowhere to be seen. Had it been deliberately removed to support the
presumption of a Japanese conspiracy? And if so, by whom?

I drifted back into the conversation. "Obviously there is
nothing more we can do here," Mr. Bullock was saying to John.
"Do you require anything else this evening, doctor?"

"Oh, it seems like a decidedly poor time to ask," John
mumbled.

"Please, Dr. Watson, I am at your disposal. What do you
want?"

"I should be grateful for any recommendations of a good
breakfast eatery."

After jotting down his suggestions on a scrap of paper
and handing it to John, Mr. Bullock accompanied us to the lobby
and engaged a buggy to return us to our hotel room. Once there, I
had every intention of confronting John about the photograph, but
the events of the day conspired against me, and I was simply too
exhausted to pursue the matter. It would have to wait until my
mind was clearer.

I arose the next morning refreshed, but also quite raven-
ous. "Breakfast is beginning to sound like an excellent idea," I
told John.

"Where is that list of restaurants Bullock gave me ..." he
muttered, searching through his pants pockets, "...ah, here it is."
He handed me the note and I read off the list of eateries, and then
stopped cold. I was no longer looking at the writing, but rather the
paper itself, which was yellow. Turning it over, I saw letters printed
on the back — *ducator* — letters that conveyed no meaning whatsoever, unless one had read the full inscription on the hand bill:
Caroline Adams, Educator. It was Bullock who had spirited away
the evidence of the flier, but why?

"John, what do you know about Mr. Bullock?" I asked.

"Very little, except for his work, which is practically all
he talks about," he answered. "That and politics, particularly that
Labor party that he and the mayor represent."

"Labor party?" I said, suddenly feeling cold.

"Yes, United Labor Party, or some such. 'The party of
the working man,' he calls it. The party of the unions, if you ask
me. Do you know that Bullock claims that virtually every workman in the city belongs to one trade guild or another? Amelia, are
you all right?"

I realized I was cradling my head between my hands, trying to keep my mind from spinning away. "Yes John," I said,
"though I fear we must postpone our breakfast and seek out that

police sergeant immediately."

Within the hour, we were sitting in an office at the city's police headquarters and speaking with Sergeant Kellin. "That is quite a story," he said, gravely, after I had laid out my speculations, "but what proof is there?"

Unfortunately, none at all I was about to confess, when Mr. Bullock chose that moment to burst unannounced into the meeting. "Dr. Watson, Mrs. Watson, I got word that you were down here," he said. "Is there anything I can do for you?"

An idea flashed through my head. "Oh, no thank you," I began, "I was just telling the sergeant of the notion that I had this morning regarding the murder. You see, while you were in the rooms of the murdered woman last night, I spoke with her neighbour next door, Sally Probert, who remembered seeing a workman in the building, carrying a length of pipe."

"So?" Bullock said. "She probably saw a plumber."

"But the water had not been shut off, she said. Obviously there was no plumbing work done, so what was the man doing there? Then I remembered that Sergeant Kellin wondered how the sword could be brought up to the room unseen, and suddenly it occurred to me that it could have been concealed in the pipe brought up by the workman."

"Go on," the aide encouraged.

"Well, Sally stated that she could positively identify the man if she saw him again, and since I've been told that all the workmen in the city are registered with a trade guild, I presumed it would be a simple matter to find the man by going through the guilds. In fact, the sergeant agreed to take Sally to the headquarters of the plumbers' union first thing tomorrow morning to begin the search." This last bit of information was complete news to Sergeant Kellin, who indeed faced me with a quizzical expression. But a sly wink of my eye bought his continued silence.

"Indeed," Mr. Bullock said, his smile looking a bit forced. Turning to the sergeant, he added: "And you are going to follow up on this lead?"

"I'm sure the mayor would expect as much from me," Sergeant Kellin answered.

"Keep me informed of your progress." Mr. Bullock then spun around and left the room.

Turning to me, the sergeant said: "You never mentioned that the woman could identify the plumber."

"That is because I just made it up," I admitted. "I was baiting the trap, and pray God it works."

I was still silently praying some thirteen hours later as John (who had spent most of the day happily giving interviews to the press about his years with Sherlock Holmes), Sergeant Kellin, three officers and I crouched uncomfortably in the darkness of Sally Probert's bedroom.

"Are you sure he will act tonight?" John asked.

"He has no choice," I replied. "If Sally is to be silenced before she can identify the workman, it has to be this evening."

As though responding to a cue, footsteps were heard in the hallway outside, followed by the metallic scratching sound of the door lock being circumvented.

"Quiet, everyone," Sergeant Kellin whispered, as the outside door slowly creaked open. A large silhouetted figure made his way into the bedroom and stood over the prone figure in the bed. After a few breathless moments, a voice from the outer room called: "Hurry up!"

"I can't do it," the shadowy figure moaned, "not again." A second shadow then rushed into the bedroom and wrenched something from the other's hand. Raising the object high, the second man plunged it into the form on the bed.

"Now!" the sergeant shouted, and the policeman closest to the room light switched it on. Standing near the bed, a deadly Japanese dagger still clutched in his hand, stood Mr. Bullock, while the large man behind him looked on, terrified. Upon realizing he had been trapped, Bullock tore back the blankets on the bed to reveal a pile of pillows arranged in the form of a person.

"We thought it would be best if Sally Probert spent the night in another room," I explained.

"I arrest you both for the murder of Caroline Adams," said Sergeant Kellin.

"He forced me to!" the large man suddenly blurted out.

"Shut up, Mordecai!" Bullock spat.

"To the devil with you, I won't!" the man Mordecai cried. " Bullock said she was an enemy of the party and standing in the way of its goals. He told me that if I helped him eliminate a thorn — that's what he called her, a thorn — I'd never have to worry about money again. But if I didn't help him, I'd be finished in the union, I'd never work again. I've got a family to support and, God help me, I did it." The man sunk to his knees and started to weep.

Bullock regarded the weeping man with disgust then met our eyes with defiance. "I hope you are not expecting such base weakness from me. I regret nothing. The enemies of the Union Labor Party are to be stopped at all cost."

"And the mayor," Sergeant Kellin said, keeping a revolver trained on the killers, "is he a part of this too?"

"That is the irony," Bullock said, smiling bitterly, "if Schmitz knew I was doing this, he would probably shoot me himself."

More policemen arrived to take the weeping plumber and the crazed government official away, and once again, John and I returned to our hotel in a fair state of exhaustion. Even so, I knew I could not put off the confrontation any longer. I had to know the truth. "Before we retire, John, there is something we must discuss," I said, opening my handbag and withdrawing the photograph, which I set down before him.

"Good Lord, where on earth did you get this?"

"It was delivered yesterday. Why have you never mentioned this before?"

"This? I suppose I felt it wasn't important enough."

"Wasn't important enough?" I cried. "Your first wedding?"

John stared at me open-mouthed. "My God, you're serious, aren't you?" he asked, shaking his head. "Oh, Amelia, is this why you have been acting so strangely towards me lately? Come sit next to me and let me explain," he entreated, and I did so. "When I was barely out of school I accompanied a friend of mine named Jimson to America. We were two young lads thirsting for adventure and convinced we were going to find our fortunes in the gold country of California. Alas, we were about twenty years too late. We soon found ourselves stranded here with no money and few friends. Jimson wrote his family, asking for money so we could return to England, but until it arrived we had to eat. We each found odd jobs. Mine you see here."

"As someone's husband?"

"As a photographer's model. I had become acquainted with this photographer chap who for some reason thought that I looked like the perfect young husband. He also knew Caroline, and he posed the two of us in costume and used the photo as advertisement for his studio. After I returned home, Caroline and I exchanged a friendly letter or two, but she was certainly not my wife."

For the second time in as many days I was rendered speechless. When I finally found my voice, it was to utter: "I am the stupidest creature on earth. How can you possibly love me?"

"It is quite easy, really," he said, taking me in his arms.

"Darling, is there anything else from your former life that you have not told me? Anything at all?"

In a fleeting instant, John seemed to age ten years, and his eyes took on the unbearable sadness of memory. "Yes, Amelia, there is, but it is still too painful to talk about. Someday I will tell you, I promise."

However long, I would wait.

THE ADVENTURE OF THE THREE VERNERS

Letter to Mrs. Elizabeth Newington from
Mrs. Amelia Watson September 18, 1905

My dearest Beth —

I truly apologize for my complete silence these last several months. I assure you that I have not dropped off the edge of the earth, though once I relate to you the events that have transpired this past summer, you will perhaps understand why it has been so difficult for me to take up the pen.

It is no exaggeration to say that my world, if not the foundation of my very being, has been turned upside-down and rent in a thousand pieces. Let me reassure you that this distress has not in any way been caused by John, who continues to be the same devoted and caring (if occasionally exasperating) man who stepped into my life two adventurous years ago. Nor, oddly enough, has it been caused by Mr. Holmes, whose presence in our lives has been mercifully sparse since Christmas, owing to his enthusiastic launch of a second career. I have been sworn to secrecy regarding his present activities, which are being carried out under an assumed name. Let me simply say that John's oft-stated belief that the theatre lost a great performer when Mr. Holmes chose to dedicate his life to detective work has proven quite astute.

This is not to say that Sherlock Holmes has no bearing in the events that I am about to relate, for he has, even though he himself does not realize it. The true culprit in this matter, if there can be said to be a culprit, is my late father.

To start at the beginning, I am sure you recall that relations between my father and myself were not always smooth. There were times when he could be a martinet of stunning proportions.

You may remember his stubborn opposition to my being part of the amateur theatre, feeling it was not the sort of activity in which a proper young lady should be engaged. He at least tolerated my decision to become a governess, although he never let me forget that he felt the only role for women in society was as wife and mother.

(Have I ever told you of his last words? After he had suffered his final attack on the street, I rushed panic-stricken to the closest surgery I could find, which happened to be that of Dr. John H. Watson. We raced back to the place my father had fallen and upon seeing John, he looked up and uttered: "Thank God, Amelia, you've found a man at last, and I approve of your choice," then died. John, of course, did his best to comfort me, and you know the rest. But I digress.)

Father and I were never closer than during the last few years of his life, after I had moved in to take care of him. I am truly glad to have had those years. Even so, there always remained a fissure between us, which while dormant much of the time, became noticeably wide whenever I tried to speak of Mother. At the very mention of her name, Father became distant and uncommunicative, as though he still blamed me in some measure for her death. I knew I was not the only person in the world whose mother had died in childbirth, though my father had a knack of making it seem so. Or so I thought.

The train of events that caused the earth to spin backwards began on a day in early June, at which time John was once more absent, away in Cardiff regaling the Welsh with stories of his emprises with Sherlock Holmes. One day, as I was sorting through the meagre stack of mail I had just received, I noticed an innocent looking letter from a solicitor named Dennistoun Peale. Upon reading it, I learned that I had been summoned to the reading of the will of someone named Montague Verner, a name I had never heard in my life!

My first thought was that it was a mistake, and promptly dispatched a telegram to the solicitor informing him so. But the next day, I received a return telegram assuring me that there had been no error, and that all would be explained at the reading, which was to take place three days hence. If for no other reason than curiosity, I knew I must attend.

I arrived at the Tudor Street office of Mr. Peale at the appointed day and time to find that three others had preceded me. One was a woman of middle years who demonstrated a regal, if not haughty, demeanor. She was introduced as Hermione Verner, the widow of a Dr. Ralph Verner, who had been the only son of the deceased. The other two were the late Mr. Verner's niece and nephew. Douglass Verner, whom I judged to be roughly thirty years of age, was raven dark and blessed with a rakish grin. His sister, Mrs. Rachel Erskine, appeared somewhat younger, though more careworn. She, I learned, was the wife of a local shopkeeper. Despite her sombre appearance, she proved to be the most immediately outgoing of the three Verners.

"Did you know my late uncle?" Caroline asked me in a hushed, slightly hoarse voice, perhaps made so by the tightness of her high collar. I was forced to admit that I was as puzzled by my presence there as she. Mrs. Verner said nothing, though she continued to stare at me, as though trying to turn me to stone.

I was, in fact, still attempting to reason out the situation out when Mr. Peale emerged from an inner office and entreated us to be seated around a long table. As we were taking our seats (the Verners all together on one side, myself on the other), the widow remarked, in a voice tinged with ice, "The old man died nearly two months ago, why did we have to wait so long for the will to be read?"

"There, there, Auntie," Douglass Verner said, "I'm sure Mr. Peale has his reasons."

"Indeed I do, Mr. Verner," the solicitor announced, seating himself at the head of the table.

The reason for the delay, according to Mr. Peale (whose lugubrious, plodding delivery would have put a turtle to sleep), was the result of a stunning deathbed declaration on the part of Montague Verner. "It was believed, by me at least, that you three, Hermione, Douglass, Caroline, were his only living heirs," the solicitor droned. "However, his own testimony has revealed the existence of another."

"Another?" Mrs. Verner questioned. Then locking me in a frigid gaze, she added: "Surely you cannot mean this creature."

Rather than answer her uncivil challenge directly, Mr. Peale instead announced: "Before I continue with the reading of the will," he began, "I would first like to read a letter written in my presence by Montague Verner, and entrusted to me mere hours before his death." He carefully unfolded a sheaf of papers, spread them out before him, and with painful slowness donned a pair of spectacles. After clearing his throat, he read: "Let no man think I am proud of what I am about to reveal. I cannot undo the damage that I have inflicted upon another human being as a result of my pride, though as I see the darkness approaching, I must do whatever I am able to make amends, however insignificant the effort may be. The parish records of St. Tristan's acknowledge the births of only three children to the Verner family within the past half-century: my son, Ralph, who has preceded me in death, and Douglass and Caroline, the children of my sister Sophia. This, alas, is a lie."

Here he paused dramatically, allowing us to absorb the pronouncement, before continuing to read: "There was a fourth child, a girl, born to my other sister, Rachel, who was not wed at the time. As scandalous as I considered that to be, and as great an affront to the good name of Verner, even I would not have sought for her the judgement that the Almighty Himself delivered for her sin — death, as the result of giving life to the child."

As you can well imagine, Beth, my mind was beginning to reel at the implications of this deathbed confession.

"My pride at the time would not allow me to acknowledge the child, yet neither could I bring myself to simply leave it as a foundling on the doorstep of the church. I confess that selfish interests in protecting the family name, coupled with genuine grief over my sister's sudden death, conspired to obscure my judgement. I therefore turned to a trusted friend, a man who had once saved my life in the thick of battle, Bertram Pettigrew — "

(At the mention of my father's name, my breathing all but stopped!)

"— and asked him for his advice as to what to do with the child. His answer both surprised and relieved me: *Give the child to me*, he said, *and no one will know*. I later learned that Major Pettigrew's wife had suffered the premature death of a child only some months before, a tragedy that continued to prey upon her mind until her own passing, barely a year later."

How can I begin to describe, Beth, the feelings of confusion, puzzlement, and loss that were overwhelming me at that moment! If only John had been there to provide a comforting arm — a vain hope, I knew, since spouses were seldom welcomed in the readings of wills. As I struggled to think clearly in the face of such shock, I realized that the three Verners were eyeing me with expressions ranging from wonderment (Caroline) to outright horror (the widow).

"Pettigrew took the girl and raised her as his own," the solicitor went on, "even after the death of his wife, at no time revealing to her that she was indeed an heir to the house of Verner. He went so far as to send me dispatches concerning her, though each of these I destroyed out of fear that someone else might stumble upon them and learn the family secret. As the decades passed, I remained secure in my believe that I had made the correct decision. Now, however, as I rapidly approach the Day of Judgement,

I realize that my soul has been left wanting. With this testament, therefore, I am instructing my friend and solicitor, Mr. Dennistoun Peale to use any means to discover the girl's whereabouts and, if she still be alive, attempt to make up for a lifetime of preterition. If these words are being heard by any of my heirs, it is an indication that he has completed this task."

With that, Mr. Peale carefully refolded the pages, removed his glasses, gestured towards me and declared with great portent: "I give you Amelia Pettigrew, now Mrs. John Watson, the long-lost daughter of Miss Rachel Verner, and niece and heir to Montague Verner."

The widow's eyes narrowed. "Do you mean to imply that we are expected to share our inheritance with her?" she asked coldly.

"That was the late Mr. Verner's wish," the solicitor replied.

"She is our cousin, then?" Douglass asked, his grin now seeming quite forced.

Mr. Peale nodded.

"In that case, how do you do, cousin?" Caroline said.

"Honestly, I do not know," I answered. "Please understand I am quite taken aback and do not know what to think. I had no idea, none at all, that I was not the natural daughter of Bertram Pettigrew."

While I was stammering unintelligently to my newfound cousins, Mrs. Verner was muttering: "John Watson, why does that sound familiar? Something to do with Ralph." She was quickly silenced by Mr. Peale's query: "Would anyone like to hear the will itself?"

I will spare you all the legal skimble-scamble, Beth, and get straight to the heart of the matter. The three Verners were each remembered in the will with substantial amounts of money (apparently, Montague Verner was a man of considerable means), which led me to believe that I was in line for the same. Try, then, to imagine my utter shock upon hearing that I was not to receive an equal share, but rather the bulk of the Verner estate, including a town house near Belgrave Square and a country home in Nottingham! My very breath seemed to evaporate in my lungs, leaving my entire body hollow and void. I tried to speak, but could not be heard over the objections of Mrs. Verner.

"You know very well that address in Belgravia belongs to me," she informed the solicitor. "Montague promised it to Ralph years ago."

"Yes, Auntie, but Uncle Ralph is dead," replied Douglass, who despite his veneer of calm, seemed quite shaken.

"Which makes the property fully mine by law," the widow declared, victoriously.

Through it all, Caroline had remained silent, though curiously, each angry word from her aunt caused her to wince and raise a hand to her throat, which was obscured by the ruching of her high-collared shirtwaist. The gesture appeared to be unconscious.

"What evidence to we have that this woman is indeed who she claims to be?" Mrs. Verner was demanding.

"I - " was all I could get out before Mr. Peale took over. "Actually, Mrs. Watson has not made any claim whatsoever," he said. "Rather, I am putting forth the claim on her behalf, based upon information that came as a result of a thorough investigation. Furthermore, permit me to point out that Mrs. Watson is a blood relative of Montague Verner, whereas you, Hermione, are related only through marriage."

Believe me, Beth, when I say that the look Mrs. Verner gave the solicitor would have frozen fire itself. Mr. Peale, however, pretended not to notice. In fact, I sensed that he might actually be enjoying having the upper hand on Mrs. Verner and relishing her indignation.

At long last, Caroline Erskine spoke up. "However shocked or distressed we are regarding this," she said, "Mrs. Watson must be more so. Perhaps, Aunt Hermione, we should let her come to terms with the situation before we attack her."

"The shock is not simply from the inheritance," I struggled to say, "but also from learning that my father was not really my father, and that my mother ..." Try as I might, I was unable to prevent the onrush of tears. I continued to battle the sobs, unsuccessfully, until Mr. Peale offered me the comfort of his private office until such time as I was able to compose myself. Thanking him, I rose and stepped to the door.

"I will come with you," Caroline said, following me in and closing the door behind us. "This must be incredibly difficult for you. May I call you Amelia?"

"Please do," I said, finally managing to control my river of tears. "And I trust I may call you Caroline." Even as she smiled, I observed that her face was marked with some inner sadness.

"I hope you will not think too badly of Aunt Hermione," she said. "Since the death of Uncle Ralph, she has been out of sorts. I am sure she did not mean all of the rude things that she said."

No, only a few of them, I thought, but said instead: "Yes, I am sure my appearance here was quite a shock to her. I can only offer my apologies for inadvertently upsetting your family in such a time of sorrow."

"Please don't apologize," she said. "I liked Uncle, but I cannot say I was close to him. In fact his bequeathal to me was more than I had expected."

"What do you plan to do with the money, if I may ask?"

Her face clouded over and she unconsciously touched her throat again. "Surely you realize that it will not be my money, but rather my husband's. That is the way things work."

Examining her throat more closely, if discretely, I thought I detected a trace of a purple mark underneath the white ruching. Perhaps it was a birthmark, about which she was sensitive. "Is anything the matter with your neck?" I ventured.

She looked startled. "No, why?"

"I've noticed you touching it, as though it was sore. If you need it examined, my husband is a doctor and — "

"No, I'm fine," she interrupted, suddenly rising and turning away. I knew I had struck some kind of a nerve, but of what sort I was not yet certain.

Once I had fully recovered from my emotional outburst, Caroline and I returned to the outer office to discover that Mrs. Verner had already left. Mr. Peale began to make a vague apology for her behaviour, but I cut him short, asking: "What would happen if I were to refuse the inheritance?"

"Refuse it?" the solicitor said. "There is no reason you should refuse it, Mrs. Watson. However, if you were to do so, your share of the estate would be divided amongst the three remaining beneficiaries. I am familiar enough with the will Mr. Verner had filed prior to your inclusion as his heir, to distribute the assets in accordance with his wishes. If it is care of the property that concerns you, though, you would be far better off accepting the inheritance and then selling it to one of the other heirs."

Douglass Verner's eyes brightened. "I would certainly be willing to entertain such an idea," he chirped.

"Let me think it over this evening," I said. "I shall notify you tomorrow, Mr. Peale, regarding my intentions."

With that, Beth, I left the office, and how grateful I was to get out! As I flagged a hansom, my mind still spinning, I wondered what the best course of action would be.

By that evening, I had made up my mind.

It was sometime after nine o'clock, as I was peacefully sitting and rereading *Nicholas Nickleby*, savouring each and every gloriously contrivance of the plot, when the telephone jangled. Missy answered it and then summoned me. "Someone from the solicitor's office, ma'am," she said. Taking up the telephone I heard a strange voice say: "Mrs. Watson? My name is Caldwell, I'm an associate of Mr. Peale's and I'm afraid something has come up regarding the will. We need to see you at our offices at once."

"At this hour?" I protested.

"I am sorry, madam, but it is rather urgent."

"Oh, very well," I said, then rang off. I informed Missy that I had been summoned to a lawyerly meeting, grabbed my jacket and hat and set out, arriving at Tudor Street some twenty minutes later. Immediately I noticed something suspicious: Mr. Peale's office was dark. If he and his associate were in there awaiting me, they were doing so without the benefit of light. My instincts told me to turn and run. If only I had listened to them.

As I continued to inspect the windows of the darkened office, I heard a voice call, "Mrs. Watson? Over here."

"Who is there?" I called back, seeing no one. Then a large, figure silhouetted darkly against the night out onto the walk.

"It's Caldwell, ma'am," the figure said. "Come with me."

"I think not," I told him, starting to back away.

In a matter of seconds, the man was upon me, holding me fast and forcing me into a pitch-dark alleyway beside the building. I felt a powerful hand tighten around my throat, all but blocking off my wind!

"Let ... me... go!" I attempted to demand, though the words only came out as a hoarse croak.

"Not until I've had my say," the brute replied, backing me up against the brick side of a building. There was not enough light to see his face, though I could feel his hot, onion-scented breath panting on me. Since his words had implied that his intention *was* to let me go, I ceased fighting. "That's better," he said. "Now, you do as I tell you and you won't get hurt. Tomorrow you're going to tell that lawyer Peale that you intend to make no claim on that will. You understand? You are giving up your part of the inheritance lock, stock and barrel, or else."

"Or else what?" I croaked.

Gripping my throat with extra force, which nearly propelled me into unconsciousness, he replied: "Or else you might have to think about writing a will of your own."

The man suddenly removed his hands from me and I sank down to the ground, coughing and wheezing. "This is no idle threat, my girl," he cautioned. "I don't want to hear that you've accepted the estate." A moment later he was gone, having disappeared into the darkness. I have no idea how long I remained in the dark alley before venturing out to hail another cab to take me home. Once there, I'm afraid I alarmed poor Missy by staggering through the door and practically passing out on the floor. She raced to make tea for me, which burned as I drank it, but which ultimately soothed my aching throat

"Who would do such a thing?" she demanded indignantly, and as I sipped, I tried to formulate an answer to that question in my own mind. The beast who had attacked me was too large to be either Douglass Verner or Dennistoun Peale. Yet it had to be someone who knew about the will. Furthermore, his implied threat to me revealed that he was in a position to learn of my decision regarding the inheritance.

In an instant, I realized that there was only one person it could have been. My suspicions were further confirmed by the reflection that greeted me from my mirror as I prepared for bed.

The next morning, after carefully dressing, I set out for what was going to be a busy day. First I stopped at Mr. Peale's office to inform him of my intentions, and to obtain other information pertaining to my co-heirs. Next I travelled to Scotland Yard, where I asked to speak with Inspector Laurie, who was an acquaintance of mine. After a break for lunch, over which we discussed our plan of attack, the two of us made our way to a small furniture shop near Pall Mall.

Posing as disgruntled customers, we entered the store and demanded to see the owner, Mr. Colin Erskine, who quickly materialized from the back. Taking one look at me, he ushered us into his office. "So, what can I do for you?" he asked, affecting an artificial smile that completely failed to disguise the cruel cut of his mouth.

"I have come to inform you that I will not accept the inheritance, Mr. Erskine," I said, my voice still slightly hoarse from the previous night's attack on me. "Or should I say, Mr. Caldwell?"

"I'm afraid I don't follow you," he replied.

"I've no interest in playing games," I fired back, angered by the wretch's devil-may-care attitude. "I do not like your sort of game, anyway." I loosened my collar to reveal the bruises on my neck, which were identical to the marks I had detected on the throat of his wife, Caroline, which she had worked so diligently to conceal. The thought of what other physical abuse he had subjected my young cousin to turned my stomach. "Your hand made this mark, so do not bother denying it."

He did not bother denying it. Instead he turned to Inspector Laurie — who had not as yet identified himself — and said, "I suppose you're the husband, brought here to try and defend the lady's honour, is that it?"

"So you admit to attacking her?" Inspector Laurie asked.

"I admit nothing," Erskine replied, "except that I could wring your neck, too, any day of the week, so don't get cocky with me, my friend. Now, is that all? I'm a busy man."

"That is not all," I said. "I want you to understand that your attempt to choke the life out of me had nothing whatsoever to do with my decision. Montague Verner spent his entire life denying my existence, I am merely returning the favour and leaving his judgement to a higher court than I could possibly affect. What's more, I do not need a fortune in possessions and a town house in Belgravia. I am quite satisfied with my life as it is. Can you say that, Mr. Erskine?"

He was silent for a moment, then asked: "Have you explained your decision to the lawyer?"

"I have."

"Then good day."

"Our business is not quite finished," I went on. "There is still the matter of your criminal assault on me."

"You can't touch me for that and you know it," he sneered.

"Perhaps I could," Inspector Laurie said, flashing his identification under the nose of the stunned Erskine.

"I thought you were her husband!" Erskine cried.

"I am Mrs. Watson's friend," the inspector replied. "Would you still like to try and wring my neck?"

The merchant's face went pale. "What are you going to do?"

"Were it up to me, you would already be incarcerated," Inspector Laurie said. "However, Mrs. Watson has told me that she has no intention to press charges."

"I appreciate it, ma'am," Mr. Erskine said. Now it was *ma'am*!

"You are not welcome, I assure you," I replied, "and my willingness to let the matter drop rests entirely on one condition: that you never lay a filthy hand on my cousin Caroline as long as you live. Like it or not, Mr. Erskine, I am now part of your wife's family, and if I ever see a mark on her again, or even so much as hear that you have touched her, I will not hesitate to call on Inspector Laurie."

"And it will be my pleasure show you how accommodating our fine London gaols can be," the inspector added.

"Now we have finished," I said, and without another word, I turned and marched out of the shop, followed by Inspector Laurie.

John returned home a fortnight later, by which time, thank heavens, the bruises on my neck had vanished. So had a large portion of my belated anger at my "father" for having died without first breaking the truth to me himself. I decided not to inform John of the events that had sent my mind and soul reeling, and that vow I have kept.

Heavens, Beth, but this is a long letter! Perhaps I should turn it into a book and publish it. But the tale is not quite over yet. Please bear with me a little while longer as I tell you of the unexpected, almost unbelievable finale to this affair. And if you are not sitting down already, you may want to.

With John back home, our lives returned to normal (more or less), and remained that way until a little over a week ago. We had just returned from an evening of the theatre when he blurted: "Amelia, what would you think if I proposed to retire from my medical practise?"

Needless to say, I was quite startled by the suddenness of it. "Heavens, dear, what would you do with yourself?" I asked him.

"I believe could write and lecture full time," he said, his eyes positively dancing with enthusiasm. "You know I have been getting more and more requests for speaking engagements, and I have also been thinking about tackling a full length play centering around my exploits with Holmes. What do you think?"

I didn't quite know what to think, and told him so, after which I innocently asked what he planned to do with his practise, which has been increasing as a result of his growing celebrity.

"Sell it, of course," he replied. "What a pity that Dr. Verner is dead. He could buy it from me again."

Had I heard right? "Did you say *Verner*, dear?" I asked, trying to sound casual.

"Indeed, a chap named Ralph Verner bought my old practise in Kensington some years back, while I was still living with Mary."

My jaw dropped as I finally comprehended the reason Mrs. Verner thought she recognized the name John Watson.

"The curious thing was," he went on, "that some time afterwards I learned that Holmes had actually put up a portion of the money for him."

"Mr. Holmes helped to purchase your practise? Why on earth did he do that?"

"It seems that Dr. Verner was a distant relative of his. I suppose it proves that blood really is thicker than water, even for someone like Holmes."

I have, of course, never been struck my a moving train, though the realization of what John had just confided in me was hopefully as close as I shall come to the experience.

"A distant relative of *Mr. Holmes*?" I cried.

"Yes, they are all descended from a French painter named Vernet."

At that moment, Beth, to my eternal shame, I fainted away like the witless heroine of a penny dreadful. The next thing I remember was John reviving me with foul smelling salts. "I had no idea you would take it this way, Amelia, forgive me," he pleaded. "I will not sell the practise of my keeping it means that much to you!"

How could I explain to him, Beth, that the reason for my faint was not his desire to retire, but the almost inconceivable discovery that *I was a blood relation to Sherlock Holmes*! Once I recovered from my swoon and the shock that accompanied it, however, I began to laugh. Before long I was reduced to such a state of helpless hysteria that John grew worried and prepared a draught for me.

So, my dear Beth, I now confide in you this privileged information. I have no intentions of ever informing John or "Cousin Sherlock" of my discovery (perhaps secrecy is a Verner family trait). Some days back, however, for reasons I still cannot precisely explain, I was suddenly consumed by the need to tell *somebody*. I found myself signalling the telephone exchange operator for a private number in Whitehall. After an unearthly number of rings, a familiar voice answered curtly, "Holmes."

"Mr. Holmes, this is Amelia Watson."

"How are you, madam?" crowed Mycroft Holmes, Sherlock's elder (and slightly more personable) brother, whom, I have learned, is a vital member of His Majesty's Government. "What can I do for you?"

Taking a deep breath, I related the entire story of the three Verners, and awaited his response. After what seemed like an hour of silence, he intoned: "Welcome to the family, my dear. Permit me to quote you a price, should you ever wish to buy your way out."

I laughed to the point of embarrassment, then cut off the line.

As the result of opening a letter from an unknown solicitor, I have acquired a new aunt, who is quite horrid; a new male cousin, whom on most days seems as indifferent as cooked rice; a new female cousin, who has already becoming a dear friend (never to replace you, of course, Beth), even though she is married to a reprehensible lout; a once-respectable husband who now harbors a desire to write and produce melodramas for the theatre; and two distant relations who happen to be the most idiosyncratic men I have ever encountered in my life.

There are times, Beth, when I have awakened at night, wondering if I should pursue Mycroft Holmes's offer to buy my way out of the family. Having already given up a sizeable inheritance, however, I would more than likely have to take up a collection to raise the necessary amount.

May I put you down for a pound?

Yours ever,
Amelia

ABOUT THE AUTHOR

Michael Mallory is the author of more than fifty short-stories, mostly in the mystery, crime and horror genres, and some 200 articles covering topics that range from writing techniques to children's television. In 1998 he received one of the first Derringer Awards from the Short Mystery Fiction Society for his story, "Curiosity Kills" (first published in MURDEROUS INTENT MYSTERY MAGAZINE). His kid's thriller, "Night Shocker," was published by Baronet Books as part of the "FrightTime" series. Outside of the mystery fiction field, Michael is the author of the book "Hanna-Barbera Cartoons," published by Hugh Lauter Levin Associates, and is an internationally recognized authority on animation. Michael has also served as a show writer for Disneyland and other theme parks, and scripted the large-format, stereoscopic 3-D film "Haunts of the Olde Country," which enjoyed a five-year run at Busch Gardens, Williamsburg, Virginia. A former broadcaster and stage and television actor, Michael makes his home in Southern California.

COVER ARTIST

Tom Sito is an animation artist who's credits include the hit films "The Little Mermaid," "Beauty and the Beast" and "The Prince of Egypt." He is currently co-directing "Osmosis Jones" for Warner Bros.